PERFECT TIMING

Boyington's attack plan called for four Lightnings to attack the bomber while the rest of the squadron engaged the escorting Zeros. When he reached the target point, Layton and his squadron climbed quickly to 20,000 feet and started to circle.

Layton barely had time to check his watch when he spotted the Japanese air convoy. At 10,000 feet, the bomber and its escort turned in a leisurely maneuver, unaware they were being watched. It was all as Boyington had planned.

Layton ordered his men to attack.

THE BLACK SHEEP SQUADRON

The Hawk Flies on Sunday

By Michael Jahn

Based on the Universal Television Series
BLACK SHEEP SQUADRON

Created for Television by
STEPHEN J. CANNELL

Adapted from the episodes
"The Hawk Flies on Sunday" written by
FRANK ABATEMARCO
"Divine Wind" written by
DONALD BELLISARIO
and
"Hotshot" written by
DONALD BELLISARIO

BANTAM BOOKS · TORONTO · NEW YORK · LONDON

THE BLACK SHEEP SQUADRON:
THE HAWK FLIES ON SUNDAY

*A Bantam Book | published by arrangement with
MCA Publishing, a Division of MCA Inc.*

Bantam edition | April 1980

ISBN 0–553–13645–3

Published simultaneously in the United States and Canada

*Bantam Books are published by Bantam Books, Inc. Its trade-
mark, consisting of the words "Bantam Books" and the por-
trayal of a bantam, is Registered in U.S. Patent and Trademark
Office and in other countries. Marca Registrada. Bantam
Books, Inc., 666 Fifth Avenue, New York, New York 10019.*

chapter

1

BOYINGTON PEERED DOWN through a break in the altocumulus clouds which blanketed the sky, and immediately regretted doing so. If he hadn't looked, he wouldn't have seen the destroyer. It was escorting two Japanese supply ships along the south coast of Shortland Island toward the enemy base on Ballale. He'd have to attack, and leading his fourteen Corsairs against a Japanese fleet destroyer in her own waters wasn't his idea of a routine patrol. Still, it had to be done.

He pressed his throat mike against his larynx. "Vella La Cava, this is Black Sheep One."

The radio crackled and a faint voice came out of the headphone. "Go ahead Black Sheep One."

"La Cava, I have a Japanese convoy—one tanker, one freighter, one destroyer as escort. I make it two miles south of Shortland Island bearing zero six zero, speed approximately 15 knots. We are attacking."

The base station repeated the information and thanked Boyington, who signed off to the accompaniment of a chorus of protests from his squadron.

"C'mon, Pappy," a voice said. "We can't take on that destroyer by ourselves."

"It's suicide," another said.

1

Boyington sighed. "This isn't going to be any big deal," he said. "I just want to put a few holes in that tanker down there. She's probably carrying aviation fuel for Harachi to use against us."

"I guess if you put it that way," T.J. said, "it doesn't sound that bad an idea."

Like some other members of the Black Sheep Squadron, T.J. had been shot down by Tomio Harachi, the leading enemy ace whose personal struggle with Boyington was one of the highlights of the battle for the Solomons. And like all American fliers, T.J. would do whatever was necessary to keep Harachi and other Japanese pilots out of the sky.

"I don't like this any better than you guys," Boyington radioed, "but we have to do it. We can't be sure the Navy can get something here fast enough. They may not even have a sub in the area. So we'll attack in two groups. Gutterman, take your planes and keep the destroyer occupied. I'll take my birds after the tanker. We'll make one pass and one pass only, so it better be good. Aim for the tanks. Let's see if we can't make a little bonfire down there."

"Roger, Pappy," Gutterman replied.

"T.J. and French, fly high cover. I don't want to find any meatballs waiting when we come back up."

The two men acknowledged the order, broke formation and climbed to 24,000 feet, high enough to keep watch over the approaches to the area. As the Black Sheep dived toward the targets, the destroyer opened up with all its guns. Twelve Corsairs dived through a wall of flak as Gutterman led his wing off to starboard, raking the destroyer from stern to bow and diverting the attention of its gunners away from Boyington.

Relatively unopposed, the Black Sheep leader and

the five planes following him poured hundreds of rounds into the tanker. Japanese crewman scrambled for cover, while a lone machine gunner aft of the bridge tried without luck to stop the American planes. As the Black Sheep climbed up and away from the murderous flak thrown up by the destroyer, oil spilled from numerous holes, covering the decks of the tanker and making it impossible to stand.

The fourteen planes made a rendezvous at 20,000 feet and circled.

"Anybody have problems?" Boyington asked.

"I've got a little flak damage to the canopy," one man reported.

Another had a bullet hole in the engine cowling, and a third was nearly out of ammunition. All in all, these were hardly major problems.

"Okay, you meatheads," Boyington said, "there's nothing to worry about, but we'll head home all the same. We'll swing past Choiseul, then cut across the Slot to La Cava."

Boyington led the formation out of its circling pattern, and had just set course for the large island between Bougainville and Santa Isabel when his headphone erupted with a loud war whoop from Jim Gutterman.

"Pappy! The tanker!"

Boyington looked down in time to watch a gigantic orange-red fireball fill the sea where the tanker once rode. It lit up the cloudy day and sent charred bits of metal flying hundreds of yards.

"That's beautiful," Boyington said as the radio filled with happy voices. "But it's gonna attract flies, if you know what I mean. Let's get the hell out of here before every Zero on Bougainville comes after us."

He set a new course, straight home this time, and,

followed by the rest of the Black Sheep, cruised straight down the Slot to their home base on Vella La Cava.

Even before America entered World War II, Greg "Pappy" Boyington had become an ace. He'd quit the Marines to fly for Claire Chennault and the Flying Tigers in Indochina, where he quickly shot down six Japanese planes. After Pearl Harbor, Boyington rejoined the Corps, and in 1943 was assigned to the Solomon Islands. When Guadalcanal was taken, the airstrips there and on Espritos Marcos made the entire chain of islands available to the recently introduced F4U–1 Corsairs. Then, when Vella La Cava was taken, Boyington asked for and received permission to organize the 214th fighter squadron with the island as a base. He peopled it with a strange mixture of rejects and screwballs, and turned them into the terrors of the South Pacific. Boyington shot down five planes on the Black Sheep's first mission, making himself a double ace almost before the squadron was in business. Soon he had become a popular hero at home in America. Boyington had a knack for staying in the headlines. The newspapers loved him, not only for his fighting ability but for his stunts. A renowned brass–baiter, Boyington performed feats normally seen only in Erroll Flynn movies. One time, the Black Sheep circled the gigantic enemy air base at Rabaul, New Britain, while Boyington verbally abused the Japanese over the radio, challenging them to come up and fight. When they obliged, the Black Sheep flamed twenty of them. Before he was shot down and taken prisoner early in 1944, Boyington rolled up 28 kills, making him the top Marine Corps ace of the war.

From Vella La Cava, the Black Sheep sortied daily into the Slot. That was the 50 by 250 mile strip of open water between the two lines of islands that made up the Solomons. From Guadalcanal on the southeast to Bougainville on the northwest, the Slot was a daily battleground for Allied forces as they island-hopped up the archipelago. All through 1943, American fliers struggled to keep their Japanese counterparts from raining death and destruction on Allied men and supplies. To that end, Boyington was happy with the day's mission; anything that kept enemy pilots out of the air saved American lives.

After arriving safely at Vella La Cava, without interference from Japanese planes, Boyington handed over the squadron to the mechanics. For once, repairs were minimal. Accustomed as they were to having the Corsairs returned riddled with holes, the mechanics were surprised and pleased. Flak damage to one cowling and one canopy was nothing. Tired but happy, the Black Sheep looked forward to an evening of no greater consequence than seeing who would win the Yankees–Red Sox game and testing the new shipment of scotch.

The 214th base was a mixture of rough tin–roofed wood huts and tents. A broad dirt runway flanked by palm trees separated the men from the jungle. On the other side of the base, a narrow path ran through a piece of woods to the naval base, hospital and beach. The Black Sheep had a three–story control tower but seldom used it, preferring to run all business at either the small radio shack or the Sheep Pen, which was their version of an officers' club.

The evening at the Sheep Pen was spent in the way most evenings were. There was universal displeasure with the new shipment of scotch and a long argument over whose bullets did the most damage to the tanker off Shortland Island. A mock fight grew out of that argument, and it was only settled when Boyington threatened to beat up all the participants. The Black Sheep relaxed with a debate over the evening's ball game, which Casey, off in the radio shack, was struggling to pick up on the short-wave. The game would be rebroadcast the following night on Armed Forces Radio, but waiting 24 hours to hear the results of a ball game was not for the purist.

Casey summed up the squadron's feelings before tucking a bottle under his arm and retiring to the radio. "I mean, you have to decide what's really important," he said, as if the fact that half the Japanese air force was trying to kill him mattered less than who hit a baseball over a fence half a world away.

The Black Sheep eventually drank the evening into oblivion, and retired to their tents reasonably happy men. The Allies had taken half the Solomons. San Remo, the latest island to fall into American hands, was scheduled to be graced with an airstrip courtesy of the Seabees. On Vella La Cava it was possible to sleep soundly, for if a Japanese raid did come, it probably would be a mild one. There were much more important targets than Vella La Cava.

Boyington fell asleep, accompanied as usual by a bottle of whiskey and his white bull terrier, Meatball. At night, the sounds of men and machinery faded. The quiet hum of an occasional generator and the far off crackle of the short-wave radio were overwhelmed by the whistling of insects and the cries of argus pheasants and hornbills alarmed by foraging groups of wild pigs. The natives had long since retreated into the highlands, there to continue their age-old manner of life, regardless of the war. But the animals ignored the Marines; they came right up to the perimeter of the field at night, just like the oil palms and foul-smelling rafflesia which at war's end would reclaim the La Cava airstrip as if it had never been there.

At four in the morning, Casey still tended the short-wave. There was much to be gained in knowing the score of a ball game before everyone else did, especially on a tropical island filled with men who had little else to do with their money but gamble. Casey had to fiddle with the fine–tuning almost constantly in order to keep the signal strong enough to hear. So when Roy Weatherly hit the O–and–2 pitch over the left field wall to lead the Yankees to a 4–3 victory over the Red Sox, Casey smiled and shut off the radio. With a final, rueful glance at his empty bottle, he shut off the lights and stumbled out of the radio shack. With luck, he'd sleep for a few hours before being roused out of bed to fly the morning mission.

Casey was halfway down the dirt strip leading to the tent city when he heard a faint droning. He looked up at the northern sky, and although he could see nothing, immediately recognized the sound.

"Oh, hell," he said.

The noise of the out–of–synch engines was unmistakeable, and annoying as a million mosquitos. Harachi might have been the terror of the Slot and Nagumo the brilliant Japanese admiral preparing the defense of Rabaul, but it was Washing Machine Charlie who had gotten the Black Sheep's goat.

In his nightly raids, the pilot of the light Japanese bomber rarely hurt anyone. Washing Machine Charlie only dropped a few small bombs and usually they fell in the jungle. But his out–of–synch engines drove the Black Sheep crazy. The Japanese pilot had the effect on the squadron of a dentist gunning his drill for ten minutes before going to work on a tooth. He must have known it, too, for he always circled the island at least twice before dropping his bombs.

The men of the squadron poured out into the night, yelling obscenities and brandishing .45's, M-1's —anything that would shoot. Even Andy Micklin, the Black Sheep's maintenance chief who generally disdained battle, was outraged. He emptied his automatic in the direction of the sound. The rest of the squadron joined him. For a moment, the camp reverberated with small arms fire, as some distance away two bombs made craters in the damp jungle soil.

"Put those engines in synch!" Micklin yelled, chewing angrily on the stub of a cigar as the bomber flew away.

"Casey!" Boyington said, "send out a couple of guys in the morning and see if you can find where the bombs landed. Maybe the bum killed us something edible."

As the men trudged back into their tents, Boyington sat on the edge of his cot and noticed with chagrin that Meatball had taken advantage of his absence to occupy the whole bed.

"Move over, dammit," Boyington snarled.

The dog grumbled but didn't move. Boyington sighed loudly and pushed the terrier to the far side of the cot, then twisted his own body around it as best he could. It was an uncomfortable position, but Boyington was getting used to it.

"I doubt Patton's dog gets treated this well," he muttered, and drifted back to sleep.

chapter
2

DAWN BROKE on another hot morning. Winter or summer, it always seemed hot in the Solomons. The only way to cool off was to run into the ocean, at the risk of being a meal for sharks, or to climb to an altitude of 20,000 feet, at the risk of being a target for bombers.

Bob Boyle walked down the path from the Sheep Pen to the flight line, scowling all the way. Jerry Bragg's snoring had kept him awake until Washing Machine Charlie flew over. After that, Boyle was too angry to sleep. So he spent a few hours working on the old spotlight in the machine gun nest adjoining the taxiway. Neither the spotlight nor the gun had been used in action, for Vella La Cava was small enough to have been declared totally free of Japanese stragglers. As a result, both had fallen into disrepair, with the machine gun nest turning into a lover's lane for those Marines and nurses who wanted privacy but weren't willing to risk the jungle.

Boyle had emptied out the old whiskey bottles and worked on the spotlight until he got it functioning again. It took several hours in all, but this was preferable to lying in his bunk without being able to sleep. And when it was all done and he had gotten ready for the day's mission, the other pilots didn't appreciate the work he put into it. He'd gotten nothing but scorn over breakfast, and, to top it all off, Carlson the chef burned the eggs again.

So when Anderson sidled up with a complaint, Boyle was outraged.

"I'd give anything for a good night's sleep," Anderson grumbled.

"With who?" Boyle snapped.

"Anyone . . . just so I get eight hours without . . ." He imitated the sound of out–of–synch aircraft engines.

"You just got the engines," Boyle said. "I got to listen to Bragg cut wood all night. But tonight's gonna be different, I'll tell you that."

"Are you really serious about shooting down Washing Machine Charlie?"

"Of course I'm serious. I'm gonna shoot him down, then I'm gonna shoot Jerry Bragg. I want to get some sleep one of these nights."

"You're as crazy as they come," Anderson said, wandering off in search of someone who would listen to his gripes.

Boyle kept on walking towards the parked Corsairs. Down the strip, he could see his renovated machine gun nest, the spotlight hooked up to the base electrical system and ready for action. He was still admiring it when Boyington and several other men caught up with him.

"Hey Bob," Boyington said, "I hear you didn't get much sleep last night."

"Who did?" Boyle snarled.

"Washing Machine Charlie . . . after he was done with us."

"Yeah, well, that's gonna end tonight. As soon as he shows up again, he gets his."

"What are you going to do?"

"You see that old machine gun emplacement down there?" Boyle asked, pointing at it.

Boyington said that he did.

"I fixed it up last night. I cleaned it, lubricated it and put in two belts of ammo."

"Who's gonna fire it?" Boyington asked.

"I am."

"Bob, you're not a machine gunner."

"So I'll learn," Boyle said. "Somebody has to do something, Pappy."

"How do you plan to find the target?" Boyington asked. "He doesn't exactly advertise where he is."

"You see the spotlight? I fixed that up, too, and hooked it into the base wiring. It's strong enough to pick out Washing Machine Charlie."

Boyington shook his head sadly.

"Who's gonna run the spotlight while you fire the machine gun?" he asked.

"Jerry," Boyle said, indicating Bragg.

"Not on your life," Bragg shot back.

"If I have to stay up, you have to stay up," Boyle snapped.

"I don't have trouble sleeping."

"Sure you don't! You're too content knowing your damn snoring keeps everyone else up!"

"That's enough," Boyington said, laughing. "We're on this rock to fight the Nips, not each other. Try and keep that in mind, would you?"

"I'm still gonna shoot that guy down," Boyle insisted.

"What you'll do, if anything, is give Washing Machine Charlie something to aim at. The second you turn on that light, he'll have a target, which he's never had before. The thing that's saved us until now is his aim. Which reminds me." Boyington turned his attention to Larry Casey. "Did you find his craters this morning?"

"Yeah, about a quarter mile north of the strip."

"Did he get any wild pigs for us?"

"No, just downed a couple of palm trees and an ironwood."

"There's not much we can do with that," Boyington said ruefully. "Did you manage to get that ball game from the States?"

"Yeah," Casey replied brightly. "I finally tuned it in. The Yankees won it in the ninth . . . four to three on a homer."

Boyington grinned. "Great! Now we can get even with those Seabees for watering down that scotch."

"How are we gonna do that?" Bragg asked innocently. Despite several months with the Black Sheep, he had failed to learn the ways of the con man. Boyington shook his head in disgust.

"I stayed up last night to pull in the broadcast out of New York," Casey explained. "Espritos will have the delayed broadcast of the game tonight, and we know the score. Yankees four, Red Sox three."

"Oh," Bragg said, catching on, "oh!"

"You'll be all right, Jerry," Boyington said. "All you need is a little sleep."

"I don't have any trouble sleeping," Bragg said, earning himself another dirty look from Bob Boyle.

The Black Sheep started to fan out to their planes. The Chance Vought F4U–1 Corsairs were ominous looking birds, with thick snouts that pointed up towards the sky even when at rest. Their 2,000 horsepower Pratt & Whitney radial engines drove the planes at upwards of 400 mph, and the six Browning machine guns held nearly 2,400 rounds of ammunition. Even Boyington was still impressed by them. As he headed for his plane, the corporal assigned to the radio shack came running up waving a piece of paper.

"Message from Colonel Lard, sir," he said.

Boyington took the slip of paper and read it. He looked puzzled.

"The mission's off," he said.

"We're not going to Choiseul today?" Bragg asked.

"No."

The Black Sheep turned and started back toward their tents.

"Thank God," Anderson said. "Maybe now we'll get some sleep."

"We're going to Espritos Marcos instead," Boyington told them.

General "Nuts" Moore was a short, stocky man who wore leather flight jackets and always carried a cane. A fine pilot, he never let the cane out of his sight since the time when, flying an air show over Shanghai, the wings tore off his biplane fighter and he managed to parachute safely to the ground, waving his cane and whooping like an Indian. Moore was not only Boyington's commander-in-chief, but his sponsor and protector as well. The General was a get–the–job–done Marine. He'd put up with almost anything as long as it contributed to winning the war. In contrast, Thomas Lard, the colonel who was Boyington's immediate superior, tried to do everything by the book and practically slept with his nose in the regulations. He was perpetually aghast at the Black Sheep's behavior, and sometimes he had the impression that both Moore and Boyington had been placed in his path as tribulations he had to endure. All he knew was that he was unable to do much about either of them.

So on that day Lard was annoyed because there had developed a great deal of activity which he knew would involve him with both Moore and Boyington. General Moore had been called to an emergency meeting, and Boyington had been summoned to Espritos Marcos. For the General to be away at a time when the Black Sheep had been recalled from the Solomons to the Hebrides augured badly for Lard and piqued his curiosity. As he watched Moore stuff his briefcase with papers, Lard grew more and more inquisitive.

"Where's Boyington?" Moore asked without looking up.

"On his way, sir. We just received his confirmation of your order."

"You mean that he actually confirmed an order? I wonder what's gotten into him."

"I don't know, sir," Lard said. "Maybe he thinks coming here will be a vacation."

"If I know Greg," Moore snorted, "it will be." He slammed his briefcase shut and looked up. "Is my transportation ready?"

"Yes, sir. Your jeep is outside and the PBY is waiting at the airfield."

"What about the Air Corps Squadron?"

"The Army's sending its best. Layton's 70th. They should be here within the hour."

"They would have to make this a joint service venture," Moore grumbled, walking to the door.

"Sir?"

"I mean it must be important, to have the best Army and best Marine outfits in on it."

"What do I tell Boyington when he gets here?"

"There's nothing to tell. Just try to keep them from wrecking the place until I get back."

Lard was no longer able to control his curiosity.

"General," he pleaded, "what's going on?"

"When I know, you'll know," Moore snapped as he turned and walked out the door, leaving Lard confused and apprehensive.

Six hours later, General Moore walked into a brightly lit conference room at an Allied base near Brisbane, Australia. He exchanged greetings with old friends and acquaintances: two admirals from Pearl

Harbor, an Army general and two captains from military intelligence. Moore's glass was filled, and he sat down to hear what was important enough to bring him away from the front, across so many miles of sea.

It was Admiral Balder, finally, who spoke.

"As you know, Moore," he said, "we've been playing tag with Japanese naval codes for some time. Now, the British have come up with something of a coup—a device which hopefully will allow us to read a lot more of the enemy's dispatches than we've been able to in the past."

Moore nodded his head appreciatively.

"To make it short, we've picked up a transmission of some importance. Tojo's planning a defense of their remaining islands in the Solomons based on Bougainville. To direct this last ditch defense, the Jap Navy is bringing in Admiral Shigota."

Moore sipped his drink in silence. Shigota was the best the enemy had. He'd been in on the planning of the attack on Pearl Harbor, and only fate and the blundering of a front-line commander prevented his repeating the feat at Midway. Let loose in the Solomons, there was no telling what he could do.

Admiral Balder cleared his throat and made his point. "Yesterday we decoded another Jap transmission. It appears that friend Shigota will be making an inspection of the airstrip on Bealle, south of Bougainville. He'll be flying in a Betty bomber, escorted by a small contingent of fighters. Apparently, the enemy has extraordinary confidence in its fighter capacity. Anyway, Moore, we've decided to send Army and Marine planes to Ballale . . ." Balder cleared his throat with deliberate portent . . . "with the intention of shooting down his plane."

chapter
3

WHEN THE BLACK SHEEP landed on Espritos Marcos, it was just before noon. By the time the planes taxied to the tie-down area and were made secure, it was time for lunch. While the members of the squadron went off in search of food and drink, Boyington sought out Colonel Lard. He found the colonel on the way out of his office, just about to climb into his jeep.

"Colonel . . ."

"Boyington," Lard said stiffly, "good to see you."

Boyington paused, expecting Lard to say more, but the colonel got into his jeep and started the engine.

"Uhh . . . Colonel, you said for me to report . . . but you didn't say why."

Lard didn't know what it was all about either, but didn't want to have to admit it.

"Well, for the time being," he said, "consider it a vacation."

"A vacation?" Boyington said in astonishment. "Colonel, are you all right?"

"Perfectly. Now, if you'll excuse me, Major, I have to do something."

"So do I, and I think it's gonna be at the officers' club bar. Why don't you join me?"

"Why this sudden interest in my thirst, Boyington?" Lard asked suspiciously.

"I'll answer that if you'll tell me why my squadron has been brought here just to have a vacation."

"I doubt that's the only reason," Lard said. "But it will do for the time being. The General will call you shortly to offer an explanation. Until that time, Boyington . . . please try not to wreck the joint."

Boyington felt it was too good to be true. Lard had never given him such liberty before. There had to be something wrong.

"What's the catch?" he asked.

"Major," Lard said in exasperation, "just go and have a good time, would you? Don't put the drinks on my tab, but enjoy yourself just the same. And please . . . *please* don't break anything."

He put the jeep in gear and was gone. Boyington watched the vehicle until it was out of sight, lost amidst the maze of hangars, warehouses, office buildings and barracks on the headquarters island. Then Boyington shrugged and ambled off, his hands in his pockets.

"If I can't get a straight answer," he grumbled, "at least I can get a straight scotch."

The Officers' Club at Espritos Marcos was a good deal larger and fancier than the Sheep Pen on Vella La Cava. A new juke box played a Duke Ellington tune while several couples danced. The walls alternated photos of military aircraft with travel posters showing the Grand Canyon, Yosemite and Cape Cod. A long bar was lined with Army, Navy and Marine personnel, and dozens of bottles glittered against the mirrored back of the bar. There was a sprinkling of nurses from the base hospital. Boyle danced with one of them who was especially good looking, although half a foot taller than he. Intensely jealous, Casey and Bragg leaned against the bar and stared at him.

"Fellas?" Boyington said, walking up and taking note of the trance they seemed to be in. Neither Casey nor Bragg responded, and Boyington turned his attention to the bartender.

"I'll have a scotch, and two more for these guys."

"Did you see that, Pappy?" Bragg asked.

"I see it."

"She's beautiful. I mean, she's really beautiful."

"What's she doing with Boyle?" Casey asked.

"Yeah," Boyington said, "I thought he was tired."

"He got his second wind," Bragg said bitterly. "Hey, Greg, did you find Lard?"

"I found him."

"Well, what is this all about? What are we doing on Espritos Marcos?"

"Enjoying ourselves. . . . He said for us to enjoy ourselves."

"You got to be kidding."

"That's what he said," Boyington shrugged. "Who am I to argue?"

Bragg and Casey hoisted their glasses in agreement, and with Boyington drank a toast to the unexpected benevolence of Thomas Lard. Many such toasts were offered as the day turned into evening and the evening into night. In the meantime, they managed to find time to eat. Bob Boyle, working on his third wind, disappeared with the nurse and returned several hours later a satisfied man. She was still on his arm, and he was very much in love. The rest of the squadron hated him, and T.J. was determined to do him one better by picking up every girl in the house.

"Evening, gentlemen," he said as he swept up to where Boyington held court at the bar.

"What'll you have, T.J.?" Boyington asked.

"No offense, but I can drink with you guys any-time."

He took a quick swallow of Casey's scotch, flashed them a thumbs—up sign, and went off in search of women.

T.J. circled the large room several times before homing in on a pretty blond nurse sitting alone at a small, round table. With a big grin, he slipped into the empty chair across from her.

"Jeannie! I haven't seen you since . . . wait, don't tell me! The MGM Christmas party in '41. You just finished that picture with Gable and . . ."

The girl smiled, flattered. "You must have mis-taken me for someone else, Lieutenant," she said.

"Are you telling me I don't know Jeannie Collins . . . the prettiest starlet on the MGM lot?"

"I'm afraid . . ."

"What in the world are you doing out here in the middle of the Pacific? I know . . . USO shows. You've been roped into coming out here and enter-taining the troops. Me, why they practically dragged me off the set and taught me how to fly a plane. Well, it's all for the war, you know."

"I'm just not her," the nurse said. "I'm sorry."

T.J. was about to carry on with the line when a Navy Captain walked up, carrying two drinks and looking aggravated.

"I guess I made a mistake," T.J. said, beating a hasty retreat.

He was a dozen feet down the aisle of tables when he practically collided with another nurse. She smiled at him, which was all the encouragement he needed.

"B.B.!" he said, "I haven't seen you since that party at Clark's!"

"Clark's?" she asked.

"Gable! The fishing lodge in Oregon. You and Clark were just back from . . ."

She laughed and interrupted him. "Jimmy," she said, "I don't know Clark Gable."

"Jimmy?"

"You *are* Jimmy Stewart, aren't you?" she asked, walking away to join another Marine who was waiting for her.

"Wise–mouthed broad," T.J. grumbled.

Anderson walked up, carrying a bottle of beer and wearing a smug expression.

"How's it going?" he asked.

"I just can't seem to find anything that suits my taste," T.J. replied.

"Yeah," Anderson said. "Sure, I'll tell you what, though, T.J. If a girl doesn't go for it, I'll make sure you get an Academy Award for this performance."

He walked off laughing. Stung, T.J. went over to a Wave who was sitting by herself.

"Mary Lou! I haven't seen you since . . ."

"Save it," she snarled.

Frustrated, T.J. went out the door. He put on his cap and was about to walk away when he spotted something in the bushes along the side of the Officers' Club. A girl was bent over, doing something. T.J. walked over to investigate and, in so doing, knocked over a cardboard box the girl had left on the ground alongside her.

An assortment of American canned goods, medical supplies and milk spilled out. Startled, the girl looked up. She was Eurasian, with long, black hair and kittenish black eyes.

"Sorry," T.J. said, stooping to pick up the stuff he knocked over. "But what are you doing?"

She resumed what she was doing, pouring milk into a shallow bowl.

"Putting out milk for the cat," she said.

T.J. picked up the last of the spilled packages and stood.

"What's your cat doing under the Officers' Club?"

The girl stood, straightened her skirt, took the box from T.J. and started off. "It's not my cat," she said over her shoulder.

T.J. ran after her and caught up a few yards down the sidewalk.

"That box has got to be heavy. Why don't you let me help you?"

"I can manage."

They were approaching a jeep, and T.J. seized the opportunity.

"At least let me give you a ride," he said. "My jeep's right here."

The girl stopped. She looked at the jeep, then at the Marine lieutenant who was still wearing his flight suit.

"Your jeep, Lieutenant?" she asked.

"Yeah," he replied.

She smiled slightly. That was all T.J. needed. He grabbed the box from her and set it on the back seat, then helped her into the jeep. Once behind the wheel, T.J. pulled a strip of wire from a pocket in his flight suit and reached under the dashboard with it. A few seconds later, the jeep roared to life.

"Do you always hotwire your jeep?" the girl asked.

"If you don't have a key you can't leave it in the ignition. It's not wise to do that. Some people will steal almost anything. My name's T.J."

"Yvonne," the girl said with a look of admiration.

"Hang on, Yvonne," T.J. said, throwing the jeep into gear and roaring off into the night.

chapter
4

THE EVENING was wearing on and Boyington was getting tired of drinking. He didn't have the energy to go looking for a woman, and anyway the matter of why the squadron was in Espritos Marcos still pursued him. Moore wasn't back on the island, Boyington knew, for the first place he'd go would be the bar, especially if he knew Boyington was in town. As he stood against the rail wondering what was going on, a dozen or so Army pilots swaggered in, looking tough and arrogant. Boyington grimaced at the sight of them. It was the 70th Air Corps, the hot Army outfit at the time, and like every other hot outfit before them, it was eager to toss its weight around.

Two of them in particular got on Boyington's nerves. Lieutenants Masters and Wright, both new aces with egos the size of their P–38's, strutted up to the bar. Wright slapped a $20 bill on the bar and snapped his fingers for the bartender.

"The Army's here, have no fear! Drinks for everyone, bartender!"

Wright took his drink and sauntered over to Boyington, Casey and Bragg.

"You fellas gonna drink with me?"

"If you're buying, we're drinking," Boyington said without enthusiasm.

The Black Sheep's glasses were refilled and Boyington prepared to drink with the Army pilots. One more, he thought, then we'll get the hell out of here. He knew he couldn't take much more of a group of kill-happy kids.

Wright raised his glass.

"Hey," he said, "you Marines are goony bird pilots, right? Christ, I envy you guys—back and forth to Australia all the time." Wright turned to his fellow Army men. "Hey fellas, hats off to these cargo pilots! They're doing a helluva job!"

The Air Corps pilots raised their glasses and drank their toast to the Black Sheep, while Boyington put a hand on Bragg's sleeve to restrain him.

"Easy, Jer," Boyington said, "he's only kidding." Then, to himself, he added: "He'd better be kidding."

Lieutenant Masters poked Wright in the ribs and pointed out Bob Boyle, who was back on the dance floor with his new girlfriend.

"My, my," he sneered.

"What a waste of talent," Wright agreed, looking at the girl.

"I didn't know the Marines had a girls' basketball team," Masters said.

Wright laughed and downed his drink. "Yeah, and with a pretty center, too."

Masters raised his voice to a point where it was loud enough for Boyle to hear.

"You think he'd pick on someone his own size," Masters said.

Boyle let go of the girl and started for Masters, but Boyington grabbed him.

"Let me go," Boyle snapped.

"Come on, Bob, let's not spend the night incarcerated."

"Huh?"

"In the brig."

"Brig or no brig, Pappy," Bragg said, "I ain't gonna listen to much more of this."

"Lard asked us not to break anything," Boyington said.

"So what? It wouldn't be the first time we didn't pay attention to him."

"Leave it to me."

Boyington looked around the room until he spotted Walter Layton, the commander of the 70th Air Corps. Layton was a standout leader, with rugged good looks and the same sort of commanding air Boyington had. Boyington grabbed a bottle off the bar and went up to him.

"Major," Boyington said, "I don't want to spoil anybody's good time, but I sense that things are getting off on the wrong foot."

"You know how it is with combat fighter pilots," Layton said.

"No," Boyington retorted. "Why don't you tell me about it? I'm buying."

He turned his bottle upside down in Layton's glass. The Air Corps major grinned.

"Why not? I heard some pretty good things about you, Boyington."

"And I've picked up a few respectable comments about you, too. Tell me, Layton, how do you manage to fly those P–38's. With those twin booms, they always make me think of two toothpicks stickin' out of the same ham sandwich."

"What about your Corsairs, Boyington?" Layton said with a grin, "I don't know how you land 'em, the way the nose sticks up in the air. You have to land 'em blind."

"The solution is to land 'em blind drunk. You know, Major. I think we could get along."

Whether or not they could was beside the point. Both squadrons saw their CO's getting along, and eased off. Boyle went back to dancing, and Masters and Wright to drinking. To help turn the customers away from fisticuffs, the bartender thoughtfully switched on the radio and tuned it to the Armed Forces rebroadcast of the ball game from New York. The ruse worked. Masters immediately cocked an ear in the direction of the radio.

"Would you turn that up a little?" he asked.

The bartender obliged. Both the Army and the Marine men clustered at the bar lowered their voices to hear the play–by–play.

"As we go into the bottom half of the ninth inning," the Armed Forces announcer said, "it's the Yankees two, the Red Sox three. Joe Gordon, batting .253, will be leading it off for the Yanks."

Boyington helped himself to another scotch and tried to look unconcerned.

"Brown winds up . . . delivers . . . the pitch is right across the letters for a strike."

Masters turned to the Black Sheep and grinned.

"The Sox have a great team this year," he said.

"Gordon swings and misses," the announcer said. "The count is oh–and–two."

"You think they've got a great team?" Casey asked.

"We're both from Boston," Wright said, "so we ought to know."

The voice from the radio kept up. "Brown's into the stretch . . . Gordon takes the oh–and–two delivery low. That makes the count one–and–two."

"I kind of like the Yankees myself," Casey yawned.

"Do you like 'em enough to put a little money on 'em?" Wright asked.

"Oh, I don't know if I like them *that* much."

"That's the trouble with Gyrenes . . . all mouth!"

"Hey, it's the last half of the ninth inning and the Yankees are losing three to two. What do you expect?"

"We'll give you odds," Masters said enticingly.

"Odds?" Anderson asked, wandering over along with Don French.

"Yeah," Wright said, "three–to–one the Red Sox win."

Casey rested a hand on Anderson's shoulder, pretending to warn him.

"Bob . . . the Yanks are a run behind and it's the last of the ninth?"

"Three to one?" Anderson asked.

"If you got enough to make it interesting," Masters said.

Anderson pulled a wad of bills out of his pocket and slammed it down on the bar.

"I think we can scare up three hundred," he said. "Is that interesting enough?"

"Count me out," Bragg said. "You guys are crazy! Betting all that money against a sure thing!"

Masters and Wright weren't thinking of betting quite as much money as the Black Sheep had challenged them to, but it was too late to back out.

"Uhh . . . yeah," Masters said. "Okay."

"Here's the pitch . . . checked swing by Gordon . . . the count is full at three and two."

The Air Corps pilots piled their money on the bar until $1200 was in the till.

"The payoff pitch," the announcer said. "Gordon swings and misses, and there's one away."

The Army men cheered, thinking themselves just two outs away from winning. Watching from the other end of the bar, Boyington and Layton smiled.

"Maybe you should talk to your men," Layton said. "My guys are doing this all the time. I'd hate to see your boys lose their money."

"I appreciate your concern," Boyington replied.

"Just a friendly warning."

Behind the bar, the radio still blared away.

"There's a ground ball deep in the hole. Lake backhands the ball . . . the long throw to first is . . . in time for the out! Red Sox fielding has been sensational this season."

The Air Corps pilots beamed happily, and the Black Sheep played at being dejected.

"The Yankees are down to their last out," the radio continued. "Ken Sears steps into the batter's box. First pitch . . . is swung on and drilled into center field for a single. Sears holds at first. That'll bring up Roy Weatherly.

"He's one for three today . . . connected for a double in the second inning. Brown gets the signal. Sets. The pitch is . . . swung on and missed! The count is oh–and–one on Weatherly. Here's the windup. The pitch. It's fouled off into the stands behind third base. That makes the count oh–and–two."

"Can we take the money now?" Masters sneered.

Anderson slapped his hand down on the till.

"Let's wait for the last out," he said.

All those at the bar leaned closer to the radio.

"Brown's oh–and–delivery is hit deep to left! Simmons may not be able to get to it!"

The crowd on the radio roared, and Boyington had trouble avoiding laughter.

"Simmons is against the wall! The ball is going . . . going . . . it's *gone!* A two–run homer for Roy Weatherly, and the Yankees beat the Red Sox four to three! If they can keep this up, the Bombers are on their way to their seventh pennant in eight years."

"Never bet against the Yankees," Casey said, scooping up the money.

Boyington tossed down what was left of his drink and picked up his cap.

"Thanks for the warning, Major," he said to Layton.

The Black Sheep grinned and counted the money as they walked out of the Officers' Club, not looking back at all on the astonished Air Corps pilots.

chapter
5

GENERAL MOORE'S QUARTERS on Espritos Marcos befitted a two–star, albeit eccentric general. There were lots of comfortable chairs and a sofa with overstuffed cushions. On the walls were photographs of his wife, his children and his three Irish setters. There was a small bar filled with bottles, glasses and an ice bucket, and Benny Goodman played softly over the radio.

Moore poured himself a bourbon and joined Boyington, Layton and Lard around the coffee table. He'd gotten back from his meeting in Brisbane early the previous morning, and though he hadn't slept much was too enthused about the mission to be tired.

"Well, General," Boyington asked finally, "how come we're on Espritos Marcos and not back on La Cava being kept awake by Washing Machine Charlie?"

"It goes this way, Greg. We're coming up fast on the Bougainville offensive. There are only a few islands between our front lines and the enemy, and we bypass those. Now, the Nips realize that once we take Bougainville, there's nothing to stop us from taking Rabaul."

"Or bombing the hell out of it, anyway," Boyington said.

"Right. And Rabaul is the biggest Jap base outside Japan. If it goes, they might as well kiss everything goodbye between here and the Phillipines."

"So they will probably put up a strong defense on Bougainville," Layton said.

"There's no 'probably' about it, Major," Moore said. "In fact, the Japs plan a strong counter-offensive throughout the entire Solomon chair."

"Great," Boyington said. "Just when I was getting used to Vella La Cava being a mile or two back from the front line."

"You got another week to enjoy it," Moore said. "We know for a fact that the Japanese counter-offensive will start in eight days."

"How do we know that?" Lard asked in surprise.

Moore cleared his throat and swirled the ice cubes around in his glass.

"Let's just say that we have information," he said pointedly.

Boyington was impressed and couldn't help but show it.

"This information . . . it's reliable?"

"Yeah, and more than that. We also got a piece of news that affects you guys more directly. Let me explain. To run their counter-offensive, the Nips are sending in Admiral Shigota. You know of him?"

"Not personally, thanks," Boyington said.

"We didn't meet," Layton added, "but one of his planes shot the roof off my barracks at Pearl."

"Then you'll have a chance to get even," Moore said. "Twenty-four hours ago we learned that Admiral Shigota will be making an inspection tour of the airstrip on Bealle. You know that island, Greg?"

"Very well, General. It's about halfway between Bougainville and New Britain. We pay our respects now and then."

"You'll get to do it again. Shigota will be approaching Bealle Sunday at 2200 hours, and so will you, Gentlemen," Moore said with a proud grin, "you're going after the Hawk!"

Boyington, Lard and Layton were stunned by the news. Killing Shigota would put a large crimp in the Japanese war effort. But could it be done. General Moore seemed certain that it could.

"You're here because you're the best shooters in the South Pacific. At 2100 Sunday, Shigota will take off from Rabaul. He'll be arriving at Bealle at 2200. Our guess is he's meeting with his head honchos there to brief them on their part in the counter-offensive."

"How do we know all this?" Boyington asked.

"I can't tell you, Greg," Moore said testily. "Furthermore, the information that we know is not to be repeated by you to anyone *at all*. Our source of information has to be protected."

"The pilots have to know," Boyington insisted.

"They'll know . . . once they're in the air. They'll be given written orders which are to be destroyed—thrown into the sea, where they'll dissolve."

"Kind of elaborate, isn't it?"

"Greg, just go along with me, would you? One of the things that comes with being a general is secrets."

Boyington nodded and went quickly across the room to pour himself another drink. When he returned, Moore had opened a small map which covered the area stretching from the New Hebrides to New Guinea. Boyington waved his glass at it.

"Bealle is nearly 600 miles through enemy territory," he said. "What about enemy coast watchers and radar?"

"There won't be much of a problem with coast watchers. After the first fifteen minutes you'll be over open water."

"And radar?" Layton asked.

"You'll be flying on the deck to avoid it."

"Flying on the deck is going to increase our fuel consumption by fifty percent," Boyington argued. "Even flying at half–speed, something I don't want to do in that area; we'd never make it back."

"Your Corsairs are being fitted with auxiliary belly tanks right now," Moore said. "Layton's Lightnings already have auxiliary wing tanks."

"That still only gives us a range of 1500 miles," Boyington said. "We'll eat up half of that just getting to Bealle. What if Shigota's late?"

"I knew Shigota when he was a naval attaché in Washington," Moore said. "He was never late for a meeting or a poker game. Besides, the local CO on Bealle is planning a big reception for him."

"What'll Shigota be flying?"

"A fast bomber, probably a Betty—with an escort of six Zeros."

"Only six Zeros?" Layton said confidently. "That won't be much of a problem."

Boyington pressed a fingertip to where the Solomons lay on the map.

"Those six may not be a problem," he said, "but we're liable to encounter sixty just getting out of the Slot. We can't fight them weighted down with fuel tanks."

"That's why we're sending two squadrons. If you're bounced, one squadron will drop tanks and fight. The other will go on."

"My boys will get him, General," Layton said.

"I didn't say *your* squadron would lead the assault, Major," Moore said sharply. "There'll be a practice mission at 0800 the day after tomorrow. The squadron that reaches the objective first will lead the assault."

Boyington and Layton exchanged competitive glances.

"What will be the objective, General?" Boyington asked.

"A destroyer off the coast of the Isles Chesterfield, 600 miles west south west of here. The first squadron to reach the rendezvous point will contact the destroyer by radio. The run from Espritos Marcos to Isles Chesterfield will approximate the run from Guadalcanal to Bealle, without running the risk of the enemy picking up on what we're doing."

"So we'll be flying out of Henderson Field on Guadalcanal for the actual mission," Boyington said.

"Yeah. I know La Cava is closer to Bealle, but having so many planes show up on your little rock all of a sudden might arouse suspicion. And while we're on that subject, you're not to tell your men anything about the actual mission until the last minute. And like I said, they won't know anything about Shigota until they're in the air."

"Understood," Layton said, and Boyington nodded in agreement.

"There's one more thing," Moore continued. "For as long as they're on Espritos Marcos, I don't want them wandering around the island. There are some Japanese stragglers in the hills and G2 thinks they may have a transmitter. The last thing we need is for the enemy to get wind of this. We'd not only blow our chance at Shigota . . . we might blow our source of information. I want your men on ice. Is that clear?"

"Yes, sir," Layton replied dutifully.

"Greg?"

"Yes, sir," Boyington said, "on ice."

Boyington said it with a grin that made the general feel faint. Upon seeing Moore's apprehension at the thought of keeping the Black Sheep in check, Layton too cracked a smile.

Boyington found his reception among the members of the Black Sheep too warm for comfort. The barracks assigned them on Espritos Marcos was stark and depressing, without so much as a pin–up or dart board to brighten things up. Moreover, they had been told to wait in the barracks for Boyington to come back from his meeting with General Moore. They assumed, wrongly, that the delay was but a momentary pause in the good time they were having. Boyington knew he'd have to tell them otherwise. The task was unappealing, and was not made any less so by the fact that they crowded around him the second he set foot in the building.

"Pappy!" Casey exclaimed. "What's Moore have to say?"

"Yeah," Bragg added, "what are we doing so far from home?"

"For the moment," Boyington replied, "we're restricted to barracks."

"Restricted?" Casey said in horror.

"To the barracks and the ball field."

"Oh, great! We can play ball all night!" Casey said.

"It's not fair, Pappy," Bragg said.

Boyington was slightly incensed. They were, after all, in a war.

"What's not fair?"

"A restriction," Bragg said. "I thought we were here on leave."

"You thought wrong. Since when do we go on leave with just the clothes on our backs?"

"But Lard *said* we were on vacation."

"At the time, he didn't know what was in the wind," Boyington explained.

"And he does now?" Casey asked.

"We both do."

"Well, Greg," Anderson said impatiently, "what the hell is it?"

"I can't tell you. At least not now."

"Come on!" Bragg protested. "We're stuck in the barracks all night and you can't tell us why?"

"It's on account of those Army creeps, right?" Boyle asked.

"Wrong."

"I'd like a shot at those guys."

"You'll get that," Boyington promised, "tomorrow. General Moore has a practice mission set up. It will be us against them."

"What kind of practice mission?" French asked.

"A rendezvous with a destroyer over open water."

Anderson was incredulous. "There's a war going on and we're playing games."

"It's not a game," Boyington said. "It's a practice mission to see who gets there first."

"How are we gonna outrun their Lightnings?" Casey asked.

"We can't," Boyington said, adding a smile. "But we might out-fly and we might out-navigate them."

The men tossed that thought over in their minds as the door swung open and T.J. sauntered in. He looked more than a little foggy; a mellow glow hung over that said very clearly he was in love.

"Good morning, guys," he said brightly.

"What's good about it?" two men snapped in unison.

T.J. was taken aback. He hadn't expected that kind of welcome.

"Where have you been?" Boyington growled.

"Unh . . . out . . . what's going on?"

"We're restricted," French said.

Suddenly T.J. was wide awake, with panic in his eyes.

"Restricted!" he shouted. "I have a date tonight!"

As a chorus of protests arose from those pilots who'd forgotten they too had made dates, Boyington stuck his hands on his hips angrily.

"Knock it off!" he shouted.

When they quieted down, he lowered his voice and spoke to them as one might address a child.

"How long do you meatheads have to be in the Corps before you understand an order? Restricted means *don't get caught!*"

chapter
6

THE ENTRANCE to the barracks compound was just across a narrow street from the base hospital, which was gleaming white with a huge red cross on the roof. Though the space between the barracks compound and the hospital was small, it might as well have been a moat filled with alligators. The gate was guarded by an M.P. with a rifle, and for all practical purposes it was an impenetrable barrier. To get the nurses in the hospital, and from there to freedom, looked impossible to Masters and Wright, who peered through the chain-link fence and berated their commander for their confinement.

"I still don't understand why we're stuck in this dump," Masters said bitterly.

"Orders," Layton replied.

"But *why*, Major? You haven't given us a reason. All we know is we're flown here on a moment's notice, restricted to the barracks, and not given a reason why."

"I can't tell you. Just believe me when I say there's a good reason for it."

Masters clenched his fists bitterly and looked out at the early evening stars. There was a lot of activity in the apparently unattainable hospital, and a few military vehicles cruised down the street towards the Officers' Club and other more interesting parts of the island. One jeep in particular caught his attention. It was the same one T.J. had hot-wired the night before. When his evening with Yvonne was over, he'd driven it a distance into the hills and hidden it in a grove of trees. To the great consternation of the Air Corps men, T.J. whipped by and disappeared down the road, with Yvonne once again by his side.

"Hey," Masters said angrily, "wasn't that one of the Black Sheep?"

Layton watched the departing jeep with clear envy.

"If they can get girls like that," he said, "maybe I'll fly with Boyington instead."

"It'd be a mistake," Wright said.

"What? Flying with Boyington? He's better than a triple ace, you know."

"I don't mean Boyington. I mean that girl who just went by. I know the little Nip. She's nothing but trouble. Said she was in love with me. It turned out all she wanted was for me to get stuff she could sell on the black market."

"That girl who just went by?" Layton asked, concerned. "You're certain it was her?"

"I never forget a body," Wright said.

"And she's Japanese?"

"Yeah, half Jap or something like that. She's real proud of it, too. I swear she's nothing but trouble, Major."

Layton thought for a moment, then shrugged it off. There were lots of multiracial girls on the islands, and if one started accusing them all of being the enemy there would be no end of it. He turned his attention back to Masters, who was still mad at T.J. for having gotten outside the compound.

"Why aren't they restricted?" Masters grumbled.

"They are," Layton said with a smile. "Evidently they're a bit more creative about it than you are . . ."

The Air Corps leader paused to make sure his men understood he'd given them the green light to attempt an escape from the compound, then turned and walked off.

"See you guys later," he said over his shoulder.

Masters and Wright smiled conspiratorially.

"All we gotta do is get by that M.P.," Masters said. "The Black Sheep did it; one of them anyway. We got to be able to do it too."

"Leave it to me," Masters said.

The two Air Corps men sidled up to the M.P., and Wright made a display of examining the man's name plate.

"Bozio, huh?" he asked.

"Yes, sir," the M.P. replied.

"That's familiar. Where are you from?"

"Pittsburgh, sir."

"Hey," Wright said eagerly, "so am I! In fact, I'm flying home on leave in a few days."

"Congratulations, Lieutenant," the M.P. said.

"Is there anyone I can say hello to for you?"

"My Mom, sir, if you would. She lives in Sewickley."

Wright pulled out a small notebook and began scribbling in it.

"I'll look her up, son," he said. "What's the address?"

"Two-eight-five Beaver Avenue. Her name's Frances."

Wright put away the notebook and smiled.

"I'll tell her what a fine job you're doing," he said.

"That's darn nice of you, sir."

Wright nodded perfunctorily and started to walk by the M.P., but the man stopped him.

"Ah . . . sorry, sir, but you'll have to stay in the compound."

"We have a sick friend to see," Wright said. "You understand, don't you, Sergeant?"

"Yes, sir, I do," the M.P. said. "But it's General Moore's orders, and I can't do anything about it."

"Let's just say you didn't see us," Wright said in exasperation.

"There's just no way, sir," the M.P. said finally. "I'm sorry."

Dejected, Wright and Masters started slowly back toward their barracks. They had gone but a few yards when from out of the middle of the barracks compound came a military ambulance, its sirens blaring. It squealed to a halt in front of the M.P., and Larry Casey, a medic's armband on his sleeve, leaned out the window.

"One for the hospital . . . serious condition," he shouted.

The M.P. stood aside, and to the astonished glances of Masters and Wright, waved the ambulance through. The ambulance roared across the street and pulled up in front of the hospital. Don French, dressed as a doctor, supervised the unloading of Bob Boyle on a stretcher carried by Bragg and Anderson, both of whom were dressed as medics.

"Careful," French cautioned, "careful."

They carried Boyle, his mouth agape and eyes closed, up the stairs to the hospital. They were met at the door by two nurses, one of whom was the tall nurse Boyle picked up the night before.

"This man needs intensive care," French snapped.

The tall nurse grinned lasciviously.

"You can rely on me," she said.

Masters and Wright glared as the Black Sheep disappeared with the nurses.

"I ain't gonna let them get away with this," Masters snarled.

"Relax," Wright said. "Our time will come."

The stolen jeep sat by a stream which ran within a hundred yards of a road leading up into a desolate jungle area of Espritos Marcos. Buttoning his shirt as he ran, T.J. chased Yvonne up the hill from the stream to the jeep.

The girl got there first and jumped behind the wheel. T.J. ran up beside her, leaned into the jeep and gave her a kiss on the cheek. It was a beautiful morning, with thousands of birds singing in the trees. T.J. was a million miles from the war.

"Whattya trying to do?" he said in mock anger, "steal my jeep?"

"How do you steal a jeep that's already stolen?" she asked.

"This jeep . . . stolen?" T.J. said, acting shocked.

"Uh huh."

"Well, maybe we should search it for goodies," he said.

T.J. walked around the Jeep giving it a long once-over. Yvonne followed him with her eyes, a smile of anticipation on her face. Finally, T.J. lifted a tarp covering a box on the back seat.

"Well, well, what have we here?"

T.J. lifted out a large box and put it on the hood. As Yvonne watched in fascination, he showed her cartons of chocolate, canned ham, fruit, candy, cookies and cigarettes. Upon seeing them, she jumped out from behind the wheel and sped round to the hood. Like a child on Christmas morning, she went through the things T.J. had brought her.

"T.J. . . . . you're incredible," she exclaimed.

"Naturally," he replied, basking easily in the glory she was handing him.

"How did you get all this? Chocolate . . . quinine . . . butter . . .?"

"I swapped for it. Only cost a case of scotch."

"A case!"

Yvonne shook her head and smiled.

"See me first next time. I'll get you a better deal."

T.J. looked at her. The thought of his new girl being an experienced black marketeer was disturbing to him.

"What do you know about trading?" he asked.

"How do you think an orphan who's half Japanese survives out here?" she asked defensively.

"I never thought about it," T.J. said.

"Americans never do."

"Hey," he said, his temper rising, "what's this thing you got against Americans?"

"The war," she said flatly.

"We didn't start it."

"No . . . you just enjoy it. It's one big drunken party, complete with native girls and moonlit islands."

T.J. let out a loud sigh.

"Wow," he said.

Yvonne melted a bit. His surprise at her tirade was an effective weapon.

"I'm sorry," she said, "but so far, I've lost my parents, a brother and a home in this war. I don't see the humor in it."

"I never said it was funny."

"You act like it's a game."

"We have to. It's that or go nuts. Do you seriously think a man can think of nothing but war, twenty-four hours a day, for several years without losing all his marbles? So we fool around. We get drunk and chase nurses. Big deal."

T.J. climbed into the jeep, took the wheel as if he was going to start up the jeep, then leaned back, his hands behind his head. Yvonne sat next to him, staring straight ahead, her anger finally subsiding.

"Do you really want to know why we do what we do?" T.J. asked.

"You're Americans."

"No. We're scared."

Yvonne turned slowly toward him.

"You don't act scared," she said.

"Who has to act? Maybe some guys aren't scared, but I think they'd have to be idiots. I've been terrified ever since I came out here, and I don't think I'm alone. Listen to this—I shot down Tomio Harachi . . . that's right, the number one Japanese ace. I blew him right out of the sky. So he survived and was back two weeks later. It doesn't matter. They put me on the cover of *Time* and gave me more medals than you could shake a stick at. Big deal. I'm still scared stiff every time I get up in that sky. So I drink a lot and I raise hell and I try to hit on every pretty girl I run across, and why not?"

Yvonne was very moved. "T.J.. . . . I never realized."

"Yeah," he said, with a slight smile, "you Eurasians never do."

She smiled, and they kissed gently.

It was late in the day, and the Black Sheep, the Air Corps squadron and nurses from the base hospital stood around an Army P–38. The Lightning was a unique bird, with two Allison engines and two booms leading back from the engine housing to the tail section. The pilot sat in a central nacelle, where he commanded four .50 caliber machine guns and a 20 millimeter cannon. The plane had a higher top speed than the Corsair and greater range, albeit less armament and maneuverability, and couldn't be carrier-based as could the Chance Vought plane with its folding wings.

Masters and Wright were showing off one of their P–38's, eager to get even for the humiliations of the previous two nights.

"Take a good look, gentlemen," Masters said

proudly. "This bird is gonna run rings around you tomorrow."

"This bird couldn't run rings around a bathtub," Boyle said.

"Are you kidding? We're gonna leave you so far behind the war will be over before you get to the rendezvous point."

"A plane's only as good as its pilot," Anderson countered. "And you guys don't exactly impress me."

"Yeah?" Wright countered. "Who do you think blew that Jap squadron out of the sky over Papua?"

"If it wasn't God, it must have been the Marines," Boyle said.

"Listen . . . we got the fastest planes and the best pilots. It's gonna be doubly hard on you tomorrow."

"Talk is cheap," Boyle snapped. "You ready to put your money where your mouth is?"

"Now you're making sense," Masters said, winking at his men.

The Army man took out a wad of bills, then went around collecting more. At the same time, the Black Sheep pooled their money and handed it over to Bob Boyle.

"Five hundred," Boyle said, counting it out. "Can you handle that action?"

Masters nodded, collecting a few more bills as he did so.

"You're covered," he said. "Who's gonna hold the money?"

"She is," Boyle said, nodding in the direction of his tall nurse.

"I am?" she asked, wide-eyed and surprised.

"You have an honest face," Boyle said with a grin, "among other things."

As Boyle and Anderson counted the money again and handed it to the girl, she grew more and more uncomfortable. A thousand dollars was a lot of money, especially on Espritos Marcos. And the nurse had gotten to know the Black Sheep well enough to realize that they weren't above winning by larceny. She definitely didn't want to be in the middle of a con game. It was tough enough being on an island full of love-starved men.

Boyington spent the better part of the afternoon and most of the evening going over aeronautical and meteorological charts. The Black Sheep and the Air Corps squadrons were scheduled to fly separate routes from Espritos Marcos to the destroyer. And though the P–38's had about 20 knots on the Corsairs, Boyington felt the Black Sheep could win the race. It would take judicious navigation and careful playing of the wind shifts, but he was convinced they could do it.

chapter
7

OVER A LONG, hard career in the Marine Corps, Andy Micklin had developed a very special manner of keeping his tent. Aside from the cot, the furniture consisted entirely of oil drums which had been washed out and inverted for use as tables or chairs. A battered radio turned out a continuous stream of sentimental music, and there were ash trays, fashioned from old tin cans, everywhere. A large coffee tin had been perforated with a beer can opener and pressed into service as a Sterno stove. Left here and there around the tent, were half-finished bottles of beer. Micklin had a habit of half-finishing cigars and bottles of beer, then leaving them someplace and forgetting where they were. He got around to finishing both cigars and beer eventually, though it often took weeks.

Micklin was a big brawny man with a regulation crew-cut and a hatred for officers that caused him to lose stripes the way most men his age lost hair. In short, Micklin took nothing from nobody and was proud of it. Before Boyington and he learned to get along with one another, several fist fights and many long drinking sessions went by the boards.

So when the corporal on duty in the Vella La Cava radio shack woke him at midnight, just after he'd fallen asleep with bottles of beer in both hands and a Dorsey tune on the radio, Micklin slammed a bottle down on an oil drum so hard it broke.

"Whattya want?" he growled.

"Sgt. Micklin, sir?" the man asked.

"Who the hell do you think I am, President Roosevelt?"

Micklin sat up, downed the other beer in one huge gulp, and tossed the empty bottle onto the floor.

"I'm sorry, sir, but there's a message for you."

"Is it from Betty Grable?"

"Uhh . . . no, Sergeant."

"Then go away before I break your neck."

The corporal shifted his weight from one foot to the other and back again.

"It's from Espritos Marcos."

"Boyington?"

"No, sir . . . Lieutenant Casey."

Micklin scowled. "I might have known," he said. "What does he want?"

"He wants you to fly to Espritos Marcos right away," the corporal said.

Micklin laughed. "Tell him to stick it where the sun don't shine," he said.

"He said it was urgent."

"So's my getting back to sleep. Jesus Christ! I just get those college boys the hell off this island for two days, and already they're bothering me again.

"I think you'd better go, sir," the corporal said. "Lieutenant Casey said he'd make it worth your while."

"Did he make an offer?" Micklin asked.

"A case of scotch, sergeant."

"Not good enough."

"He said he'd throw in two cases of beer," the corporal replied.

"What kind?" Micklin asked suspiciously.

"Ballantine, sir."

"It better not be shaken up," Micklin said, standing up and looking around for his pants.

Several hours later, Micklin strode irritably along the line of tied–down Lightnings looking for the Black Sheep. It hadn't taken the transport long to fly him from Vella La Cava, but while in the air he'd gotten around to total distrust of the deal he'd made with Casey. Micklin hated to fly; it terrified him, and all he could think of the entire way was the fun he'd have kicking butts when he caught up with the Black Sheep.

Casey was waiting for him alongside Layton's P–38 when Micklin finally arrived. With Casey were four other Marine pilots, all of whom looked around warily, fearful of being caught.

"Andy!" Casey said in a loud whisper, "you're just in time."

"Where's the booze?" Micklin snarled.

"You get it when you finish the job."

"Okay, sonny boy, I'll do it. But you better come through. Now, what am I supposed to do that's so important."

"We want you to fix this Lightning," Casey said.

"What?" Micklin asked. "I fix Corsairs, not these things."

"I don't mean fix it, I mean *fix* it. Screw it up. Sabotage the compass. Make the compass so the pilot will fly a couple degrees off course."

"You flew me all the way here to do *that?*" Micklin shouted.

Everybody looked around to see if Micklin was overheard.

"Why don't you speak up?" Boyle said angrily. "Maybe nobody heard you."

Micklin glowered, and looked like he was ready

to take Boyle apart. Casey grabbed him by the arm and led him away from the others.

"Look, Sarge . . . it boils down to upholding the honor of the Corps."

"You know what you can do with that," Micklin said.

"Okay, okay . . . I understand."

"What does my messin' with their compass have to do with the Marine Corps' honor?"

"We're flying a little race tomorrow," Casey said. "There won't be any combat . . . just practice. And we bet the Army we could beat 'em."

"Then you was stupid," Micklin snarled. "A Lightning's faster than a Corsair."

"Yeah . . . we know."

"Then what the hell are you up to? I thought you college boys were supposed to have brains."

"We only made the bet after their line chief said we'd be lucky to get our cruddy wrecks off the ground."

Anger flashed across Micklin's face, and he clenched his huge fists.

"Wrecks, huh? Where is this line chief. I think I'm gonna go over and change his shirt size."

"Hey, we want to win the dough," Casey said, "not beat the guy up. And we can win it if you'll rig Layton's compass so it's off a little. Just enough to make things sort of . . . well, fair."

Casey gave Micklin a comradely clap on the back.

"What do you say?"

Micklin mulled it over for a minute or two, alternating his gaze between Casey and the P–38.

"Wrecks, huh?" he said finally.

"Cruddy wrecks," Casey said.

Micklin smiled.

"Did you shake up the beer?" he asked.

"Huh?"

" 'Cause I hate beer that's been shaken up," Micklin said, starting for Layton's plane.

The two squadrons took off at 0800 as scheduled and set off on their respective courses. Moore had two separate courses laid out so that the pilots would not be able to see their rivals, and this would have less of a tendency to push their planes beyond the prescribed limits for long–distance missions. The courses were supposed to be equal, but Boyington—who had spent a good deal of time on the charts—had found that if his own course were slightly altered, it would have the advantage.

The Black Sheep were nearing the rendezvous point. Boyington was doing the navigating for the squadron, as Layton was for his. Although flying a few yards above the water, Boyington ran his finger again and again over the pencil line he'd made on the map stuck to his clipboard. After assuring himself that his computations were correct, he touched his throat mike.

"Coming up to the second quadrant," he broadcast. "Ready to change our heading south by six degrees."

"Ready," Casey answered.

Boyington checked his watch.

"Changing course . . . now!"

In unison, the Black Sheep banked left slightly and headed six degrees to the south for the final leg to the rendezvous point.

"Are we on course?" French asked, over the radio.

"On the money," Boyington replied.

"You sure, Pappy?" Anderson asked.

"Yeah, I'm sure," Boyington said irritably. "How

come all this concern? Most of the time, all the navigation you guys care about is how to get from the bar to the john."

"I'm tryin' to develop an interest," Anderson replied.

"Sure you are."

"I am," he insisted.

"How much is the bet for?" Boyington asked.

"Five hundred," Boyle replied.

"Even money?"

"Yeah. We conned them into it."

"That's a lot of money to spend on such a chancy thing," Boyington said.

"We got a lot of faith in your navigation, Pappy," French said.

Boyington frowned. He knew they never bet that much unless it was a sure thing or somehow rigged. Boyington felt it had to be the latter, but he wasn't certain. In any case, he wasn't going to go into it over the radio. He put the subject out of his mind and returned his concentration to flying.

The Black Sheep flew on another half hour, barely above the waves.

"Hey Pappy," Bragg broadcast, "I just saw a shark."

"Pay attention to what you're doing," Boyington said, "or you'll be sleeping with the sharks."

"Aren't we getting near the rendezvous point?"

Boyington checked his watch. "We're there," he said. "Climb to angels ten and start looking for that destroyer."

The Black Sheep throttled up and began a slow ascent to 10,000 feet. As the planes gained altitude, the sea spread out before them like a carpet. There were few clouds, and Boyington could see for miles. It took but a few seconds to find their objective. The American destroyer steamed in a slow circle, at precisely the point on the map where it was supposed to be.

"Destroyer . . . ten o'clock," Casey radioed excitedly.

"Got it," Boyington replied.

"I don't see those Army hotshots," Anderson said.

Boyington smiled as he activated his throat microphone. "Bull's eye, this is Black Sheep One."

"We read you five–by, Black Sheep One." The reply was loud and clear, and very pleasing to the squadron's ears.

"Reporting on station as of one–one–three–five hours," Boyington said.

"Roger, Black Sheep One . . . so logged. And congratulations, Major Boyington—you're first on the scene."

There was a great burst of cheering from the pilots which momentarily overpowered the radio. When it was over, Boyington resumed his conversation with the Navy radioman.

"You haven't heard from Major Layton?"

"No sir. I might add, sir, you've made half the men on this ship mighty happy."

"What about the other half?" Boyington asked.

"They bet on the Army, sir," the man replied.

chapter
8

BOYINGTON AND LAYTON sat silently for the several minutes it took for General Moore to finish reading the report on his desk and look up at them. Layton was formally polite when they met in the outside office, and Boyington assumed his aloofness was due to having lost the race. In any event, the outcome pleased the General, who grinned broadly.

"It looks like you'll be leading the assault, Greg," he said.

"Thank you, sir."

"You made great time this morning. How the hell did you do it?"

"I have a good line chief back on La Cava," Boyington said.

"Isn't that Micklin? The guy who knocked out a dozen of Colonel Bateman's teeth back in El Toro?"

"It sounds like him," Boyington said.

"You've tamed him?"

"We get along well enough. I haven't had to take a poke at him in a month."

"Good. Well, Major Layton, what happened to you today? Your planes are supposed to be faster."

"We did our best," Layton said stiffly. "Major Boyington just got there before we did, sir."

"Maybe you'd better get a line chief like Greg's," Moore said.

"I might do that. In fact, I might hire Micklin away from Major Boyington. If I see him again, I'll make an offer."

Boyington's eyebrows arched sharply.

"When have you seen Micklin? You've never been to La Cava. At least not since Micklin and I have been there."

"I saw him an hour ago, working on one of your Corsairs."

"What the hell's he doing here?" Boyington asked.

"I wouldn't know," Layton said dryly.

"I'm due at Fleet," General Moore said, consulting his watch. "I want both of you to come up with a flight plan for the mission. I'll give you my input from Fleet tomorrow and we'll put it all together."

The two majors stood as Moore left the office, then walked slowly out into the daylight.

"Let's go to the Officers' Club," Boyington said. "I'm buying."

"Being a good sport, huh?"

"Why not?"

"Boyington, do you know that one of your men is running around with a Japanese girl?"

"Sure, T.J. is. And she's only half Japanese."

"You *know*?"

"Look, you take care of your squadron and I'll take care of mine. Fair enough?"

"No," Layton said, "it's not. One of my men knew her, went out with her, in fact. She took him for a lot of goodies that she sold on the black market."

"So? We all make deals."

"Yeah, well, the rumor is she deals with people friendly to the Japanese. I have a responsibility to my men. Maybe this girl's trouble and maybe she's not. Back in the States, they're tossing Japs in detention camps just for being Japs. This girl also cons GI's into stealing stuff she can sell on the black market, and for all we know might be collaborating with the enemy. I'm not about to risk the lives of my men on her account. If *you* are, you have no business wearing that leaf."

Boyington had no defense. Layton was right in being cautious about the girl. If Yvonne was giving information to the enemy, she couldn't be allowed to learn anything about the upcoming mission.

"One more thing," Layton said, digging into his shirt pocket and pulling out a small magnet. He dropped the magnet into Boyington's palm.

"You can give this back to whoever put it behind my compass last night. Your line chief, most likely."

He walked off, leaving Boyington staring at the magnet in his hand.

Boyington commandeered a sergeant's office at the back of the barracks and used it as a combination office and bedroom for the duration of his stay on Espritos Marcos. Scattered around the room were charts of the Solomons, sketches of possible flight plans, ash trays, bottles and glasses. Boyington was at the old metal desk, drinking scotch and studying a meteorological chart of the area around Bealle when the door swung open and Andy Micklin stomped in.

"Whattya want, Boyington?" he snarled.

"You want a drink, Andy?"

"I don't drink with officers. Besides, I got things to do."

"Such as?"

"Get me a boat back to La Cava. I ain't flyin' if I can avoid it."

"Andy, what are you doing on Espritos Marcos?"

"Tryin' to get the hell off it," Micklin said.

"Did you put a magnet behind the compass on Major Layton's P–38?"

"Sure I did. Those college boys weren't bright enough to figure out how to do it themselves."

"How much did they give you?" Boyington asked with a sigh.

"A case of scotch and two cases of beer. But the beer's no good. Those college boys of yours shook it up. I hate beer that's been shook up."

"They brought you all the way here just to screw up Layton's bird?"

"That's about the size of it. Now, if you're finished with me, I'm tryin' to work out a deal with some Navy guys to ferry me off this rock."

"Okay," Boyington said. "Before you go, tell me how things are on La Cava? Is Gutterman taking good care of the place?"

"Sure . . . as good as he knows how."

"Get lost, Micklin," Boyington snapped. "And if you see T.J., send him in."

"Mr. Foul–the–Plugs? Sure, I seen him. He's outside, trying to figure out a way to mess up his plane so's it can't be fixed at all."

Boyington poured himself a stiff drink when Micklin left, and sipped it while trying to focus his eyes on the weather report for the Solomons on the day of the mission. He'd just about done it when the door opened again and T.J. walked in, looking like a teenager in love for the first time.

"You wanted to see me, Pappy?"

"Sit down, T.J. Have a drink?"

"Sure," T.J. said, sitting on the edge of Boyington's bed and watching while a drink was poured for him.

"Look, T.J., I don't want to say this, but it's become unavoidable."

"What's the matter, Greg?"

"There's a lot going on around here right now,

and it's being complicated by the fact you're seeing a girl who's part Japanese. That's making a lot of people jumpy."

"I don't understand."

"Security," Boyington said gravely.

"You're kidding."

"I wish I was."

"Just because she's half Japanese doesn't make her a spy."

"It's more than that," Boyington said.

"Well, what is it, then?"

"One of Layton's pilots used to go out with her."

"If you've got something to say, I wish you'd just say it." T.J. was starting to get angry.

"For you and me," Boyington explained, "this war is basically pretty simple. We go up in our planes and we either make it back or we don't. It's not that simple for this woman."

"Just what are you talking about?"

"She's evidently trying to make it through the war as best she can. But right now her methods make it questionable for you to . . ."

"Why don't you just come right out and say it," T.J. cut in. "You think she's a prostitute!"

"Did I say that?" Boyington snapped.

"You were thinking it."

"Dammit, T.J., I'm not going to argue with you. Stay clear of her 'till I tell you otherwise!"

Furious, T.J. leaped to his feet and glared at Boyington.

"You telling me that as my friend or as my commanding officer?"

"Any way you want to take it," Boyington said. "But I'm telling you to keep away from her. There's more in the wind than you know about, and I don't want it jeopardized."

T.J. whirled and rushed out of the room. When he left the barracks, he looked around for transportation. The jeep he'd stolen his first night on Espritos Marcos was long since gone. But there was a white hospital jeep nearby which would do just as well. He headed for it and was halfway there when Air Corps Lieutenant Wright, who was walking by at the time, stopped him.

"Hey . . . aren't you the guy who's seeing Yvonne?"

T.J. stopped and glared at the man. "Yeah . . . what of it?" he snapped.

Wright made a conciliatory gesture. "Hey, look . . . just a friendly warning. All that broad cares about is the stuff you can give her to sell on the black market. I ought to know. I . . ."

T.J. didn't wait to hear more. He hit Wright with a left cross that was good enough to knock the Air Corps pilot onto the ground. Then T.J. stormed over to the jeep, jumped behind the wheel and drove off.

It took him less than half an hour to find Yvonne, and all the while he worried about what Boyington had said and what he himself had been thinking ever since he met her. She was a wheeler–dealer, no doubt. She also disliked and distrusted Americans. In wartime, far less substantial evidence could label someone a security risk. Boyington was right, and T.J. knew that his anger came from realizing it. He had to confront Yvonne. Maybe she could say something that would put his mind at ease, not to mention get Boyington off his back.

He found her walking down a street running past the Marine PX and the Corps' executive buildings. A package, wrapped in white paper, was under her arm, and her perfect black hair swung from side to side as she walked. T.J. pulled the jeep up alongside her and jumped out.

"T.J.," she said, surprised to see him, "I thought you were going to . . ."

T.J. grabbed the package and tossed it aside. He pulled a few bills out of his wallet, crumpled them and stuffed them in her blouse.

"Why bother with the middleman? Why not just take cash?"

"T.J.," she said, shocked.

"What's the matter? Did I offend you? I'm sorry. . . . After all, you love me, right?"

"What happened?"

"They're coming down on me for seeing you. They say you might be a spy. You *do* hate Americans. You told me so."

Yvonne looked down at the ground, at once sad, angry and embarrassed. "Please, T.J., don't be like the others."

"Others?"

"The Japanese treated me like trash because I'm half French. The Americans treat me like trash because I'm half Japanese. All I'm trying to do is survive. I thought you understood that."

"I understand what you tell me. Now I'm asking you to give me something I can tell my friends. Yvonne, every time I see you you're hustling black market stuff and knocking America. Please give me something I can tell my friends to change their minds about you."

"I'm trying to survive," she insisted.

"So's Tojo," T.J. shot back.

Yvonne took the money T.J. had stuffed in her blouse and threw it in his face. Then, before he could react to the shock, she ran to the jeep, jumped into it and roared off.

"Yvonne!" he called out, as she disappeared down the street.

Angry with himself, he kicked the ground, then

ran off in search of a vehicle with which to chase her. He soon found it. A Marine Corps messenger had left his motorcycle in front of the Exec Building. In a flash, T.J. was on it and speeding away in pursuit of the jeep.

chapter
9

BETWEEN MICKLIN AND T. J., Boyington managed to
find himself in a foul mood. What he had really wanted
to do was go over to the Officers' Club and get loaded,
but instead he had forced himself to concentrate on
work, and finally had come up with a flight plan for
the mission. So he folded the paper on which he had
written the plan, stuck it in a pocket, and went into
the barracks to give his pilots hell.

The Black Sheep were sitting around the barracks,
congratulating themselves on beating the Air Corps
pilots, when Boyington stormed in.

"Whose idea was it to put the magnet behind
Layton's compass?" he yelled.

There was silence, which only made him angrier.

"I suppose Micklin got the idea all by himself."

"We all did it, Greg," Casey admitted. "We had a
bet with the Air Corps guys."

"How come I didn't know about the magnet?"

"We thought . . ."

"You thought wrong! That flight was preparation
for an important mission! Maybe the most important
mission you meatheads will ever fly!"

"We didn't know anything about that," French
said.

"Are you in command now, Don?" Boyington asked.

"No, sir."

"Where's the money you won from them?"

Begrudgingly, Bobby Boyle handed over the Air Corps' $500.

"You're not gonna give it back?"

"You bet your ass I am. Beating them out of money on a ball game isn't the same as tampering with their navigational equipment. What if Layton had run into a Jap patrol this morning?"

"There aren't any in this area," Casey said.

"This is a shipping lane. There are subs. What if he had to break off from the race, attack an enemy target, then couldn't navigate home because of the damn magnet you guys stuck on his compass?"

"I never thought of it that way," Bragg admitted.

"That's one of the reasons you're not in command," Boyington snapped, sticking the wadded-up bills in his pocket and walking out of the barracks. He'd barely gotten to see daylight when Colonel Lard's jeep roared to a halt in front of him.

"I want to talk to you, Boyington," Lard said angrily.

He got out of the jeep and waved a fistful of reports in Boyington's face.

"You know what these are? One's a report on a stolen jeep. Another's a report on a stolen motorcycle, and the third's a report on *another stolen jeep!* You want to hear the fourth?"

"Do I have a choice?"

"No! The fourth is a report that one of your men has been seen with a Japanese girl. I want to know what the hell is going on."

"You know as much about it as I do," Boyington replied.

"Did you know that Lieutenant Wylie was seeing this girl?"

"He has orders to stay away from her."

"Then you *did* know about it."

"I just learned."

"Do you have any idea how important the security of this mission is?"

"Yes, sir," Boyington said irritably.

"I want you and Lieutenant Wylie in my office in ten minutes," Lard snapped.

"I'm due at General Moore's office in five minutes to go over the flight plan."

"Then we'll talk right after that meeting," Lard said, getting back into his jeep. "Hop in."

Begrudgingly, Pappy got into the jeep with Lard and drove off.

Posted on the wall of General Moore's office was a huge map of the South Pacific, showing the Solomons, New Britain and New Guinea. Bealle was marked with a small Japanese flag. Boyington waggled a pointer at it while Lord, Layton and Moore watched.

"Once we get out of the Slot," he said, "we fly due west, just south of the Russels."

"How far out to sea will that leg of the flight take you?" Moore asked.

"About fifty miles."

"All right. That's a pretty secure area. They'd never spot us out there."

"What speed?" Lard asked.

"Two hundred," Boyington answered. "It's a bit above optimum cruising speed, I know, but with the belly tanks should be no problem."

Boyington ran the tip of the pointer along the line he'd drawn up the Solomon Sea toward the island of Bealle.

"Once we reach the point fifty miles out," he went on, "we turn north to avoid any spotting boats that might be in the area."

"So when you make your final approach you'll be coming from the west," Moore said.

Boyington nodded.

"What time do you figure to get there?" Colonel Lard asked.

"Twenty-one-fifty . . . just before he lands."

"G2 figures Shigota will travel under 10,000 to be comfortable and stay off oxygen. He's known to dislike wearing a mask."

"Where do you plan on jumping him?" Layton asked.

"Here," Boyington said, touching the tip of the pointer to a spot off the coast of Bealle. "About forty miles out. We want to meet him just when his polot is thinking about the landing."

"You've got to get him on the first or second pass," Moore said. "You can't let him get close to shore. They've got about a hundred Zeros based on that field."

"I just hope they don't get the notion to send half of them out to meet him," Layton said.

"They won't," the General replied. "Shigota will have six fighters as escort . . . no more."

"You're certain of that?"

"Yeah, I am. The Japs think of Bealle as a safe area. Their pride will prevent them from giving him greater protection. Also, our information that led to this mission comes from a source the Japs think so secure they'll never suspect we've tapped into it. Unless, of course . . ." (he gave Boyington a purposeful look) ". . . someone tells them."

Boyington shuffled his feet uncomfortably. He'd have to track down T.J. and find out what was going on with the girl.

"How's the fuel situation going to be?" Lard asked.

"It's close. We can't kid around. I figure we've got five or ten minutes in the target area at best."

"Let's hope that's all we need," Moore said. "Now, unless there are questions, I'll see you men at takeoff."

The meeting broke up and Boyington walked out behind Layton. When they reached the outside, Boyington took the wadded-up roll of bills from his pocket and pressed it into Layton's palm.

"Give that back to your men," he said to the surprised and pleased Air Corps major.

Boyington walked straight back to the Black Sheep barracks, where his men were gathered awaiting his return.

"How was the meeting, Pappy?" Bragg asked.

"The hell with the meeting. Did you find T.J.?"

Several men shook their heads, and a few others shrugged their shoulders in helplessness.

"All we know is a nurse said an M.P.'s been looking for him," French said.

"He couldn't have just disappeared," Boyington said.

"We looked everywhere, Pappy," Bragg reported.

"The beach? Did you try the beach?"

"A dozen times."

"He told me Yvonne's folks had a plantation on the north side of the island," Casey said. "But he wouldn't have gone there . . . would he?"

"If she went there, he went there. Besides, we've looked everywhere else on this rock. Anybody know how to get to the north side of the island?"

"No," Casey said, "but there's only one road to that side."

"I'll need a jeep."

"You got it," Boyle said. "I got you a good one. Brand new. Compliments of the Navy."

"How many vehicles have you guys stolen since we've been here?" Boyington asked. "No . . . don't tell me."

"Who counts anyway?" Bragg said.

"Thanks, Bob."

"You want someone to come with you?" Bragg asked.

"No. What I want you to do is think up an excuse for me if I'm not back by seventeen-thirty."

"I hope you find him, Pappy."

"You better hope so," Boyington said. "If I don't, we're all up the creek."

chapter
10

LIEUTENANT T. J. WYLIE had indeed gone to the north side of Espritos Marcos. Though Yvonne's family's plantation had been destroyed early in the war, she continued to live on it—in a small cottage that was little more than a shack. The cottage was several hundred yards off the lone road, and the path leading to it was too narrow for a jeep. She left the jeep in the bushes by the side of the road, having made a halfhearted attempt to camouflage it with elephant ear leaves and bamboo.

T.J. spotted the jeep immediately and parked the motorcycle alongside it. Then he jogged up the path, ducking low-hanging branches and vaulting thick jungle creepers.

The cottage had been painted white many years before, when it still served as home for a tenant farmer. But the paint was nearly gone, and many of the boards were far enough apart to see through. T.J. ran across the tiny clearing where the path widened to include the cottage. When he reached the door, he pushed it open and squinted into the darkness inside. As he struggled to see, the muzzle of a Japanese automatic was pressed against his temple.

"Take it easy," he said softly. "I didn't come here to hurt you."

Yvonne lowered the gun with a sigh and stepped back from the door. Her voice was sad and tired.

"Why did you have to follow me?" she asked.

"I made a mess of what I wanted to say. I have to try again."

T.J. was about to go on when he saw a Japanese soldier in a tattered old major's uniform. The man's leg was bandaged, and he lay on a makeshift bed. He looked feverish and very scared.

"What's going on?" T.J. asked.

"Who is he?" the Japanese asked in broken English.

"It will be all right," Yvonne said. "He is a friend."

"He's a Japanese officer!" T.J. exclaimed.

"He's also my uncle. So now you know why I've been trading on the black market. And why I'm bitter about Americans. I have to care for my uncle."

The man tried to bow, although he was lying down and it was quite impossible. T.J. stepped cautiously toward him.

"Major Ishiro Takashima," he said weakly, "Seventh Imperial Marines."

T.J. gave an abbreviated salute. "Lieutenant Wylie, United States Marines . . . 214th fighter squadron."

He dropped to his knees beside the bed and examined the major's leg. The look and smell of gangrene was unmistakable, and T.J. backed away from it.

"Yvonne . . . he needs medical attention."

"He won't let you take him prisoner! He'll commit sebuko first!"

"We can't just leave him out here."

"The plantation is only a few miles away. If you could help me move him to the old house, we would be safe. No one would look for us in the ruins."

"What do you mean by 'us'?" T.J. asked.

"The three of us. We could sit out the war there, T.J. They'd never find us. It could be wonderful."

"You want me to *desert?* And take along a Japanese officer to boot?"

"He's my uncle! He's not going to hurt anyone. The war is over for him. T.J.," she pleaded, "it could be over for you, too."

T.J. stood mute, trying to fathom what was going on in his life. He hadn't bargained on all this when he joined the Marines. Up to that moment, warfare had been impersonal; it had meant flying a machine which spat bullets at a target which often was so far away you couldn't see the man in it. He was startled back into awareness by the sound of Boyington's voice.

"What's it gonna be, T.J.?"

Yvonne whirled and levelled the gun at Boyington, who walked slowly into the cabin.

"Don't come any closer, Major," she warned.

"Yvonne!" T.J. exclaimed, making a grab for the gun.

She jumped away in fear, and stood aiming the weapon alternately at T.J. and Boyington.

"No!" she said. "I won't let him take my uncle to one of your prison camps!"

"He's not here for your uncle," T.J. said. "He's here for me."

"Then you better go."

"You just said you wanted me to sit out the war with you."

"That was before *he* came," she said, indicating Boyington.

"You're not making sense."

"*You're* the one not making sense, T.J." Boyington snapped. "You're acting like a lovesick kid over a girl who'd use you . . . me . . . anyone she had to, to keep that man alive."

"No!" T.J. said emphatically. "She loves me."

Boyington felt his temper rising. "Damn it," he said to the girl, "tell him."

"Your Major's right," she said softly. "My duty to my family comes first."

"Duty to your family! What about us? You and me? You just asked me to go over the hill for you, Yvonne!"

"Would you do it?" she asked calmly.

T.J. thought for a moment, then sighed loudly. There was no way he'd have deserted, for her or anyone else.

"See?" she said. "I don't ask if you love me. I know you do. But there are times when love isn't enough."

T.J. stood mute in reluctant agreement.

"Come on, T.J.," Boyington said, "we got things to do."

"Okay, Greg," he said tiredly, turning and walking out of the cabin.

Boyington lingered in the doorway long enough to point an accusing finger at Yvonne.

"We're going, but I'm gonna tell you something —if you won't get that man to a hospital pretty soon, he's gonna die."

"You haven't even looked at his wound," she replied.

"I don't have to. I can smell it. That's gangrene, lady."

"You're lying," Yvonne said, frightened.

"Do you think I'd let a Japanese officer loose on this island if I thought he'd survive?"

The girl looked at her uncle with an expression of utter helplessness. The Japanese officer smiled grimly and pushed himself up on one elbow.

"Lower the gun," he said with difficulty. "We will

go with this man. He is right. I cannot hide any longer."

"But what about their prison camps?"

"I am an officer. I won't be mistreated. And there is no point in my dying in this cabin."

Boyington called T.J. back inside, and together they helped Major Takashima into one of the jeeps. Shortly thereafter, they were speeding back down the road towards the base.

Boyington drove as fast as he dared down the narrow streets of the military base on Espritos Marcos. The stolen jeep drew stares but no M.P.'s as Boyington pushed it to the limit in his effort to get to the flight line before the combined squadrons left without him. It was 15 minutes to flight time. He'd dropped the girl and her uncle off at the base hospital, raising a few eyebrows. It wasn't often that somebody came in with a Japanese major, then left without a word of explanation. Boyington laughed at the thought of it.

"What's funny?" T.J. asked as he clung to the edges of his seat.

"I was thinking about Major Takashima. The way that doctor's mouth fell open when we carried him in, uniform and all."

"I hope he'll be all right. At least, I think I hope so."

"We'll stop back after the mission and make sure. They'll want to know the whole story anyway."

"Greg . . . the mission ends in Guadalcanal, not here."

"Oh yeah. I forgot. Well, we'll get back to Espritos Marcos some day."

T.J. nodded, but without enthusiasm.

"I don't know whether or not to be mad at her," he said.

"I'll tell you what, T.J., take it out on the enemy. If we meet any unexpected Zeros today, we're gonna need all the anger we can work up."

"Sure thing, Pappy," T.J. said with an embarrassed grin.

Boyington drove onto the airfield and made his way toward the flight line. In the distance, he could hear the sound of engines. Just down the pavement from the control tower, Major Layton was walking alone, heading towards his squadron of P–38's. Boyington pulled up alongside him.

"Ah, Major Boyington," Layton said, jumping into the jeep. "And the lost sheep. Hello, Wylie."

"Good morning, sir," T.J. replied.

"Glad you made it. Another five minutes and I'd have left without you."

"Another five minutes and I wouldn't have blamed you. How's Moore taking my absence?"

"About what you'd expect."

"Oh," Boyington said.

"He was groaning about it, so I made myself scarce. Claimed to have to pick up a new weather report. I thought that might defuse him a little."

"Thanks, Major."

"You'd do the same for me," Layton said as they roared down the rows of parked P–38's and Corsairs and came to a screeching halt in front of Moore and Lard. All three men jumped out and saluted as the Black Sheep and Air Corps pirates hedged around them.

"Where the hell have you been?" Moore snapped.

"At the tower, sir," Layton said, waving a piece of paper. "Last minute weather over the route."

Moore eyed Boyington suspiciously, then shrugged.

"Okay, Greg, let's get on with it."

Boyington gestured for the combined squadrons

to move even closer, then looked around to assure himself no one else was listening.

"In ten minutes we take off on a very important mission—the most important mission I've ever flown, and I doubt if any of you have or will ever have a more important one."

There was a hushed silence as his words sank in. All the vague references to "an important mission" they'd been hearing during the past few days were turning out to be true.

"We're flying first to Henderson. We'll refuel there and take right off for Bealle Island. You know it. We'll be flying on the deck all the way, and if we run into any Zeros, Major Layton's squadron will drop auxiliary tanks and engage them. We'll continue on to Bealle."

No one had the nerve to ask what for, so Boyington drew a breath and continued.

"Specific instructions are in your cockpits. Read them once we're over the sea and dump them. The gist of it is that Japanese Admiral Shigota will be approaching Bealle for an inspection tour today. He'll be in a Betty bomber, and we're going to give him a reception."

Both Marine and Air Corps men were too stunned to say anything.

"Gentlemen," Boyington concluded, "we're going after the Hawk."

chapter
11

THE TWO SQUADRONS made the hop to Henderson Field on Guadalcanal with no difficulty. There the planes were refueled, and after a short break took off for Bealle. There was to be radio silence all the way. As the 32 planes flew just above the waves, the only communication was by hand signal. The men had worked out a rotating system of watches; for the duration of the long flight, eight would watch for enemy planes or ships while the rest concentrated on flying. That was no small task. Flying on the deck allowed no room for error. At angels 20, one could drop 500 feet without difficulty. But at a stone's throw above the sea, any error in altitude could be instantly fatal. The air was thicker, and the sea much closer.

Boyington watched over the paired squadrons as the flight progressed. Despite not having slept, he was alert, even on edge. Flying on the deck was a harrowing task, especially when such an important mission hung in the balance. So when radio silence was broken by a frantic message from Larry Casey, Boyington felt his whole body tighten.

"Zeros . . . eleven o'clock . . . a flock of them," Casey warned.

Boyington looked to the left. A flight of about 20 Mitsubishi A6M fighters—called Zeros by Allied airmen because of the circle painted around their noses—

was closing in on the Corsairs and Lightnings from the southwest.

Another voice came over the radio. "Stand by to drop tanks," Major Layton told his men.

The P–38's were about to jettison their auxiliary fuel tanks and engage the enemy when the Allied pilots heard a voice the Black Sheep knew well coming from the radio.

"Hey Boyington . . . is that you?"

Boyington laughed. The number one Japanese ace, Tomio Harachi had long been the thorn in Boyington's side. But coming after the days of tension preparing for the Shigota mission, hearing from him was almost a relief. At least, Boyington thought, Harachi has a sense of humor. He pressed his throat mike.

"Tommy . . . what are you doing here?"

"It *is* you, Boyington. Why you flying so low? Something wrong with your plane again?"

"Nothing that won't stop me from flaming you, Rice Ball."

"We see about that, okay? You and me, Boyington?"

Boyington smiled ironically. He wanted to be the one to shoot down Shigota's plane, but he wanted Harachi more. And no one was more accustomed to the tactics of Harachi's squadron than the Black Sheep.

"Black Sheep One to Eagle Leader," he broadcast. "Do not drop tanks. . . . Repeat, do not drop tanks."

He felt the Black Sheep were better shots than the Air Corps pilots, but the latter had a faster plane with better range. Harachi's arrival simplified a decision Boyington had been trying to make.

"Eagle Leader . . . this is Black Sheep One. This guy you hear on the radio is an old friend. I think I'd better say hello. Good luck."

Perplexed, Layton responded. "Okay, Boyington . . . if you say so . . . and thanks."

"Black Sheep One to Black Sheep. Drop tanks and engage."

As their auxiliary fuel tanks fell into the Solomon Sea, the Corsairs powered up and climbed to meet the approaching Zeros. As they did, the P–38's continued on their way to the rendezvous with Admiral Shigota, flying on the deck as before.

Harachi noticed them. "Hey Boyington," he radioed, "what's with your friends? Looks like they're running away."

"You know the Army. They never stick around when you need them."

In the cockpit of his Lightning, Major Layton grinned broadly and shook his head.

The Black Sheep were outnumbered by the Japanese, but that was usually the case. The Black Sheep had beaten odds as great as four–to–one. Boyington had no reservations in meeting Harachi this time out.

The two sides engaged at 15,000 feet. The Corsairs were still climbing—an unfavorable position to be in. But the sun wasn't a factor, and a layer of wispy clouds obfuscated the situation. The Black Sheep attacked in pairs, with Boyington breaking away to attack Harachi on his own.

Their planes were distinctly marked, and the two long-time rivals found each other without difficulty. As the P–38's disappeared into the distance, Boyington and Harachi spun and dove, exchanging fire. Casey got another kill, and Bragg sent two Zeros flaming down into the sea. Anderson was pretty badly shot up by two Japanese planes, and had to retreat back to Guadalcanal accompanied by Don French. Bobby Boyle got one Zero so clearly in his sights that when he pressed the trigger the Japanese plane virtually disintegrated in front of him—blew apart so completely that Boyle had to fly through the debris, putting several spider-web cracks in his canopy.

Boyington and Harachi broke off after a few minutes. Harachi had run out of ammunition, and Boyington had a long row of Japanese 20mm holes in his left wing. The two sides parted in silence. The Japanese had lost four planes, and the Black Sheep flew back to Henderson with one Corsair in wretched condition.

When Boyington and the rest of the Black Sheep taxied to the tie-down area assigned them on Guadalcanal, General Moore was waiting. He sat on an oil drum, and when Boyington walked up tossed a beer bottle.

Boyington flipped it open and took a long drink.

"So you got ambushed," Moore said.

"Yeah . . . Harachi again."

Boyington finished the beer in a second mammoth swallow and helped himself to another from a tub of them Moore had by his feet.

"Nice of you to bring libation, General," he said.

"It's for the bunch of you. And there's a lot more where that came from if the mission is successful."

Boyington nodded appreciatively and slumped onto the tarmac, leaning against the tub full of beer.

"So how'd you get jumped?" Moore asked.

"The usual way. A flight of twenty Zeros who were heading northeast about twenty miles out. They were flying at about angels 20, probably on their way back to Bougainville after a sweep down the Solomon Sea."

"That could be," Moore said. "There was some shooting east of the Louisiades this morning—one of our convoys had it out with a pack of Zekes."

"It must have been Harachi," Boyington said. "He ran out of ammo pretty quick once we engaged. I wondered if he'd been using it earlier in the day."

"If he ran dry, why didn't you nail him?"

"I tried, General, but my right wing got pretty badly shot up and I was having control problems."

"I see."

"There'll be another day for Harachi and me. My boys flamed four Zeros, though, so the day wasn't entirely lost. That's against one Corsair more or less ruined."

"I saw that thing coming in," Moore said. "I don't know how the hell your pilot brought her home."

"He knew there was beer waiting."

"Which reminds me . . ." Moore waved his empty bottle, and Boyington handed him another. "Thanks, Greg," he said, opening the bottle and taking a drink, then letting out a satisfied sigh. "I'll tell you, this is the first time I've gotten to relax in a week."

"You gonna tell me now how you got the information about Shigota?" Boyington asked.

"Nope. You might get shot down and taken prisoner."

"No way, General. I'm too lucky."

"Yeah—lucky your ass isn't in the stockade!"

"What for?"

"Are you kidding? Try two . . . no, three stolen jeeps, a stolen ambulance, a stolen motorcycle, and I heard a rumor about a fight with half a company of Seabees."

"They sold us a batch of watered-down scotch," Boyington said quickly.

"And then there was the matter with Lieutenant Wylie's girl," Moore said.

"It turned out well enough. Major Takashima is okay, isn't he?"

"The last I heard, the doctors thought they had stopped the gangrene without having to chop his leg off."

"Good. He doesn't seem like such a bad guy."

"It will go easy on him," Moore said. "And at least we now know the girl isn't really a security risk. She will still have to be interned, of course. Wylie will have to wait until after the war."

"I doubt he's still interested," Boyington said. "Harachi took his mind off her. You know," Boyington laughed, "T.J. still thinks Harachi is gunning for him in retaliation for flaming him that time. The mere mention of Harachi's name sends T.J. up the wall."

"I don't blame him. Well," Moore said, consulting his watch, "Layton should be reaching the target point soon."

"Yeah," Boyington said, yawning after he did so. "It's a damn shame there's nothing for us to do for the next couple hours but sit here and drink."

Boyington's attack plan called for four Lightnings to attack Shigota's bomber while the rest of the squadron engaged the escorting Zeros. When he reached the target point, Layton and his squadron climbed quickly to 20,000 feet and started to circle. They'd be vulnerable to detection on Bealle radar, but if Shigota was on time his countrymen on the island wouldn't be able to do anything about the attack. And Shigota was always on time.

Layton barely had time to check his watch when he spotted the Japanese air convoy. It was banking toward the island preparatory to making a landing approach. At 10,000 feet the bomber and its escort turned in a leisurely maneuver, unaware they were being watched. It was all as Boyington had planned. Using hand signals. Layton ordered his men to attack.

The P–38's came roaring down out of the sky, spitting fire from all four guns. The Zeros dropped their belly tanks and climbed to intercept, but by then Layton and the three pilots following him in the attack on the bombers were screaming down at over 400 miles per hour. Only lucky shots could have stopped them, and the Japanese weren't lucky that day.

As the rest of the squadron peeled off at 15,000 feet to take on the fighters, Layton and three others dived straight for the bomber. The aircraft banked sharply and dove to avoid them. A row of holes appeared in the side of its fuselage as Masters connected. Above, some of the enemy fighters had taken note of the four Lightnings going after the bomber and were diving back in a frantic effort to reach them.

As his three companions swung right to stay on the tail of the bomber, Layton abruptly rolled right, dove below the bomber and then swung up on it from below, where the Zeros couldn't get him without risking a hit on the Admiral's plane. A surge of excitement swept through the Air Corps leader as the belly of the Japanese plane came into his sights and he pressed the trigger.

Round after round pounded the Betty's fuselage. Layton could see a trickle of oil, then smoke. He swung away after several metal plates were blasted off the tail section, and in a tremendous wrenching of metal, the tail section tore off. The bomber spiralled down to the sea, where it exploded on impact. Japan's greatest remaining military mind never had a chance.

chapter
12

LAYTON'S FLIGHT returned to Guadalcanal in relative safety. Only one plane had been lost—Wright's. Badly shot up in the fight at Bealle, he had to ditch in the Solomon Sea just to the west of New Georgia. But Air Sea Rescue picked him up and delivered him to Henderson Field in time for most of the party. Protecting the secrecy of the information that led to the Shigota mission dictated that any radio message from Layton announcing victory had to be a cryptic one. Thus, half way home, when the possibility of pursuit by vengeful Zeros was minimal, Layton radioed Guadalcanal with the message: "On routine patrol past Bealle Island engaged six Zero fighters, one Betty bomber. Two Zeros and the bomber destroyed. One P–38 lost. Request Air–Sea Rescue coordinates . . ." and so on.

The message may have been obscure, but it was understood perfectly by those waiting to hear it on Guadalcanal. They had gone to get the Hawk, and they had succeeded. By the time the Air Corps squadron reached Henderson, the party was well under way. It went on for the rest of the day and all the following night, spilling over from the Officers' Club to the barracks and ending in a long poker game during which nearly everyone fell asleep. The next morning found only one Black Sheep able to stay on his feet.

T.J. Wylie leaned against the chain–link fence

topped with barbed wire that surrounded the internment compound for Japanese prisoners and enemy sympathizers. He gazed into the dark eyes of the half-Japanese, half-French girl who clung to the other side of the fence, her hands touching T.J.'s.

"You left to go on a mission," she said. "How did it turn out?"

"It was just a routine patrol," he replied. "Greg only said it was a mission to get me out of that cabin your uncle was living in. How is he, by the way?"

"Better. The doctors seem pretty sure they can save his leg."

"How does he feel?"

"Okay. He's in a ward with several other officers. He feels he was taken honorably. There's no more talk of suicide."

"Good," T.J. said.

She squeezed his hand.

"T.J. I'm sorry," she said softly.

"Don't be."

"But I used you."

"You did what you had to do. You couldn't have told me when we first met that you were only trading on the black market to support your uncle who is an enemy officer in hiding."

"I guess not."

"I wouldn't have understood."

"You might have."

"We'll never know, will we?" he said, squeezing her hand back.

"Will I see you again?" Yvonne asked.

"Not for a while. I have to get back to Guadalcanal. They don't even know I'm gone. Then it's home to Vella La Cava and God–knows–what."

"After the war?"

"Sure," T.J. said, though he knew there was little chance it would happen. "Are you being taken care of here?"

"It's not as bad as I expected," she thought. "The food isn't great but it's regular . . . and at least I don't have to wheel and deal."

T.J. beckoned her closer to the fence. He pressed his lips against hers through the wire grating. "Goodbye, Yvonne," he said, softly but matter–of–factly, and walked back to his plane.

The Black Sheep, tired but happy, dragged themselves into their tents on Vella La Cava late that evening. They were home at last, after the better part of a week spent on Espritos Marcos and Guadalcanal. While they were away, Jim Gutterman had done his best to keep up the squadron's record, leading daily sorties into the Slot with an abbreviated flight of six planes. They shot down two enemy fighters and spent a long day looking for the wreckage of a United States PT boat reported lost off nearby Kolombangara. They couldn't find a trace of the small warship, and the incident went down as a contribution to the increasing number of complaints against enemy destroyer activity in the Solomons.

Boyington fell asleep easily, without bothering to glance at the paperwork piled up on his desk. He wanted nothing more than to sleep for a week, but knew it was out of the question. With luck, he could put in eight hours and make up the rest later on. Boyington was fast asleep when he heard a droning coming from the north. He opened his eyes slightly and scowled. It couldn't be! Not on the first night back!

But it was. Washing Machine Charlie serenaded the base with his out-of-synch engines as he closed in on Vella La Cava for his nightly bombing run.

Bobby Boyle had just fallen asleep when his old

nemesis woke him. He sat up on his cot, rubbing his eyes and thinking hateful thoughts. Jerry Bragg hadn't started to snore yet but was dead to the world, unaware of the sonic terror in the sky. Infuriated, Boyle kicked the side of his cot.

"What?" Bragg exclaimed, jumping up.

"It's him!" Boyle shouted.

"Who? Harachi?"

"No . . . listen!" Boyle pointed up. Bragg listened for a moment, then groaned.

"I was asleep," he said.

"So was I. And I'm gonna be asleep every night from now on, cause you and I are gonna shoot down that out-of-synch sonofabitch."

"C'mon, Bob . . . go back to bed," Bragg said.

"No. I set up the machine gun nest with a spotlight and lots of ammo. All we need is to go out there, switch on the light and shoot the bum down."

Bragg reluctantly got to his feet and pulled on his pants.

"I got to be crazy to go along with you," he said.

Two minutes later, Bragg and Boyle were out in the old machine gun nest, cranking up the equipment. It hadn't been cannibalized while they were on Espritos Marcos, which they knew was nothing short of a miracle for a wartime island. Bragg flipped on the spotlight while Boyle fed a belt of ammunition into the machine gun and brought the first round into the chamber.

Washing Machine Charlie's erratic droning grew ever nearer as Jerry Bragg switched on the spotlight and used it to search the northern sky. The beam swept back and forth as Boyle sat with his eye glued to the machine gun sights.

A moment later, the small Japanese bomber, whose engines were intentionally run at different speeds to annoy the Black Sheep, came into range. The only other sound on the Marine base was off in the jungle where, a few yards from the machine gun emplacement, a group of wild pigs foraged in the thick underbrush.

"There he is!" Boyle yelled as the bomber hove into view. He pressed the trigger on the machine gun and the air was filled with fire.

Boyle kept it up for nearly a minute, until Bragg yelled, in exasperation, "He's too high! You can't hit him! He's out of range."

"I can hope, can't I?"

"You can also be blown to hell," Bragg said, abandoning the spotlight. "We've given Charlie something to aim at. He's never had it before."

"Oh, hell," Boyle said, realizing Bragg was right.

He followed Bragg in running away from the area, and not a moment too soon. For one of Charlie's bombs landed in the jungle ten yards from the machine gun emplacement, felling trees and making a noise heard all over the base.

The spotlight went out with a loud pop, and Boyle and Bragg were knocked to the ground. Sandbags that formed the perimeter of the machine gun nest flew around them. The rest of the Black Sheep poured out of their tents, and, as they had so often before, emptied their pistols and rifles at the disappearing Japanese plane.

Andy Micklin chewed the end off his cigar and shook his fist at the sky. "If I ever get my hands on that Japanese college boy," he snarled, "I'll kill him!"

As it turned out, nobody got his hands on Washing Machine Charlie that night. He flew off, and when he was safely out of range of the Black Sheep's ire, put his engines in synch and flew home to his base in Bougainville.

Late in the afternoon the next day, Washing Machine Charlie was temporarily the hero of the day on

Vella La Cava. In his normal morning-after survey of Charlie's craters, Casey found two wild pigs killed by the bomb. The carcasses were trussed onto bamboo poles and carted to the mess tent, where Carlson took time out from burning the breakfast eggs to dress the pigs. By mid-afternoon, they turned slowly on hastily constructed spits built over smoldering fires.

The Black Sheep were well into their feast, accompanied by a complement of nurses from the nearby field hospital, when they heard the droning of aircraft engines across the field. When Boyington looked up, he saw three Lightnings circle the base and then touch down and taxi to the refueling pumps near the mechanics' shed. Their engines were shut off, and a few minutes later Masters, Wright and Layton ambled over to where the Black Sheep were having their picnic.

Boyington jumped up and shook their hands. "Sit down," he said. "Eat and enjoy yourselves."

"Thanks, Major," Layton said, "I think we'll do that." The three Air Corps men loosened their flight suits and sprawled on the ground with the Black Sheep and the nurses. Before long they were handed plates and bottles.

"Where'd you get the ham?" Layton asked.

"Oh, a Jap bomber gave it to us. He visits us every night, and this time managed to hit something useful."

"That's great," Layton said, taking a tentative bite and nodding in approval.

"What brings you to La Cava?" Boyington asked.

"Refueling. We were ordered to search the area around Kolombangara for that PT boat that's missing."

Boyington shrugged. "I don't know anything about it."

"The kid who skippers it—his old man is some kind of bigshot. Used to be Ambassador to England, I think. Anyway, he's from Boston, so Masters and

Wright are hot to find the kid. As if the three of them are the only ones from Boston in the war. The guy's named Kennedy . . . you know him?"

"Sorry," Boyington said. "We get a lot of torpedo boats in and out of here. I don't pay much attention to 'em one way or the other. Anyway, I'm surprised they've got you flying missions. I thought they'd want to send you home and make a hero out of you."

"They do. They want me to do a tour of the States to help sell war bonds."

"Are you gonna do it?"

"I don't know yet," Layton said. "On the one hand it would be nice not to have people shooting at me for a while. On the other hand, those tours are such b.s."

Boyington nodded knowingly. Ever since he'd become a triple ace, the Marine Corps bugged him periodically about helping to sell bonds. He couldn't make up his mind either.

It was then that Larry Casey, who didn't know the Air Corps pilots had joined the party, came running from the direction of the radio shack.

"Greg . . . I just tried out the new short wave antenna. . . . I think I can get the Yankees–Cleveland game tonight. We can get the score and tomorrow shoot down to Espritos Marcos and . . ."

He stopped in mid-sentence upon seeing Major Layton.

"Oh, nuts," he said.

"Nice work, Larry," Boyington said bitterly.

The Air Corps men sat in momentary silence, then broke into laughter which the Black Sheep joined.

chapter
13

THE ALLIED INVASION of Bougainville began November 1, 1943. During the month before and for a good time afterward, the Black Sheep concentrated on that island. For one thing, Vella La Cava was the nearest American airstrip to Bougainville. For another, taking Bougainville would put the entire lower Solomons in American hands, erasing the Slot as an aerial battlefield for all time. And with Bougainville runways as a base, the Allies could move on Rabaul, which was considered by some to be the Gibraltar of the Pacific.

Late in October the Black Sheep were ordered into the air to help escort a flight of B–24 bombers from Guadalcanal on a run against Bougainville. The pre-invasion softening up of enemy positions had become an everyday thing. On that particular day, the 214th were flying medium cover. Bell Aircobras were low cover, and Air Force P–38's high cover. The Black Sheep joined the formation over the Slot east of La Cava. It was an impressive sight: more than 140 planes arranged in four formations, taking up a large chunk of sky all the way from 10,000 to 28,000 feet. The objective was the enemy airfield at Buin on the southern coastline.

It seemed like a cut-and-dried matter at first, but halfway up the Slot a storm front moved in from off the Ontong Java Rise. The towering blue–grey cumulus clouds brought with them not only a cold front but the prospect that the bombers wouldn't even be able to find the target, let alone drop their bombs with anything resembling accuracy. The plane–to–plane radio channel buzzed with opinions and complaints.

"Black Sheep One, this is Blue Leader," the bomber CO called.

"Black Sheep One, go ahead, Blue."

"This is your territory. What do you think of these clouds."

"In two hours we'll have a storm, lots of rain, and a temperature drop of about ten degrees."

"What about the target? Will it obscure the target?"

Boyington consulted his map, flying with his left hand as he ran a finger over the area they were flying. "I don't think so," he replied. "You're gonna get an offshore breeze this time of day. It should keep those clouds away from the target long enough for us to get in and out."

"You're sure of that?"

"Negative, Blue Leader . . . but it usually happens," Boyington said.

"Yellow One to Blue Leader." It was the Air Corps, flying high cover in their P–38's, checking in.

"Go ahead."

"I don't like it. I don't think we're gonna find a damn thing with all this soup."

The Air Corps Aircobras added their inevitable opinion. "Red One to Blue Leader."

"This is Blue Leader. Go ahead."

Boyington thought the bomber CO sounded tired.

"We're with Yellow. I can't see the front of my bird."

The Aircobras were the lowest formation, constantly flying in and out of the clouds. Boyington understood their dilemma, but he wasn't about to give up so easily.

Sitting in the cockpit of his B–24, the flight leader watched as the dark clouds built up to nearly 20,000 feet. Everyone but the high cover would have to fly through them.

"Back to you, Boyington. Are you willing to stick it out?"

"Sure thing."

The radio was filled with the sounds of protest from the other two fighter formations. Finally the flight leader had had enough of it. The low cover couldn't see at all; the high cover couldn't see more than a few thousand feet below. Standing against them was Boyington's opinion that the storm wouldn't break over Bougainville before they had time to get in and out.

"Blue Leader to Yellow and Red squadrons. You have permission to go home. Blue Squadron will fly this one with the Black Sheep. We'll go on a bit and see if Black Sheep Leader isn't right about visibility over the target."

The other two fighter squadrons acknowledged the order, but said little else. It was as if they were too embarrassed about their reluctance to complete the mission to say more. One by one, their pilots peeled away and reversed course, heading back down the Slot towards Guadalcanal. Soon just two squadrons remained, the Blue squadron of bombers and the Black Sheep.

"I hope you're right, Boyington," Blue Leader radioed.

"Me too," Boyington replied as the planes drew ever nearer to the coast of Bougainville.

Buin was on the coast just beyond Shortland Island, where the Japs maintained spotters and antiaircraft batteries. But the storm hung over Shortland Island like a shroud, pounding it with thunder and lightning and obscuring the sound of American aircraft engines. And just out of range of the Shortland batteries, the coast of Bougainville loomed as pretty as a picture. Slowed by the offshore breezes Boyington had predicted, the clouds were taking their time arriving. The sun still shone on the target as the two squadrons closed ranks and prepared for the bombing run.

"Nice work, Boyington," Blue Leader said happily. "I have the target in sight."

"Thanks, Blue, and good shooting."

"We'll do our best. Stick with us, Black Sheep. We'll make this one a quick in-and-out."

"Acknowledged, Blue Leader. Did you copy that, meatheads? We stick by Blue squadron—that means no freelancing for kills."

"Right, Pappy," Casey replied, and several other Black Sheep added their responses.

As the American planes bore down on the target, a complex of oil and gasoline storage facilities outside Buin, a squadron of Zeros rose to meet them.

"Enemy planes, ten o'clock low," Anderson reported.

"About twenty of 'em, Greg," Casey added.

"Stay with Blue formation," Boyington again cautioned. "With any luck, we'll be on our way home before they can climb up to our altitude."

The Black Sheep watched as the B–24's swept in towards the fuel storage tanks below. Despite their altitude advantage, the first wave of Zeros did get to them, but not through the fighter screen. Casey and French got one each, and Wilkinson, a new man, picked up his first. Seeing the accuracy of the Corsairs' fire, the second wave of enemy planes tried to draw them into a fight, hoping that with the Black Sheep engaged in a dogfight, the third wave of Zeros could get at the B–24's.

But Boyington wasn't about to be drawn off. The Corsairs stuck with the bombers until many tons of destruction rained down on the fuel dump below. Flashes of fire lit up the countryside, and thick black smoke rose to mingle with the approaching clouds. A few seconds later, the deep rumble of ground explosions shook Buin as the oil and gasoline went up. Several of the Air Corps pilots cheered, and the Black Sheep joined in.

"Okay, let's get the hell outta here," Boyington said.

"You got it Black Sheep. . . . Reverse course and make for the clouds."

The B–24's and Corsairs turned and throttled up. Not one of the planes had been lost, although several B–24's had been riddled with 20mm cannon fire from the Japanese fighters. Boyington wanted to keep it that way, and he sighed with relief when the two squadrons flew into the tops of the approaching clouds and disappeared.

The Black Sheep handed the homeward–bound B–24's over to a squadron of Mustangs that would escort them back to Guadalcanal. Then the Corsairs banked right and headed for their own base on Vella La Cava. As they drew away from the bombers, the praise lavished on him by Blue Leader stuck in Boyington's mind. The fact that this offbeat Marine squadron had stuck with him when his own Army pilots would not impressed him as being great heroism. Were it not for the Black Sheep, the fuel dump at Buin would have gone on supplying the enemy, perhaps for a long time.

Consequently, Boyington was in an ebullient mood when he taxied his Corsair to the tie-down area and left it. With Colonel Lard as a superior officer, Boyington didn't get much praise. Sure, General Moore was appreciative, but the most praise he ever handed out was a fast "nice going."

When T.J. ran up, Boyington didn't suspect there was anything wrong. T.J. was an eager type, always running somewhere, and having been left out of the mission to Bougainville because his plane broke down was bound to have left him restless. Probably, Boyington thought, he'd gone to the other side of the island and fallen in love with a nurse.

"What's up?" Boyington asked.

"It's Baumann, Greg."

Boyington frowned. Captain George Baumann had been nothing but trouble ever since he joined the Black Sheep as replacement for Jim Gutterman, the executive officer. When Gutterman was rotated back to the States, Espritos Marcos sent Baumann along to fill his shoes. In one way, Baumann was very much like Gutterman. Both had bad tempers, only Baumann's was worse. Boyington wondered how he had managed to get two consecutive bad-tempered execs, when the second in command was traditionally a politician, having to get along with both the men and the CO. Baumann got along with neither. But he was a good pilot, so Boyington had decided to put up with him for as long as it took to get Gutterman back or find another exec.

"What's wrong now?" he asked.

"We flew a routine patrol to the west coasts of Rendova, Munda and Kolombangara," T.J. said. "Off Kolombangara, George spotted what he thought were two American PT boats running close to shore. I told him they were Jap picket boats, but he didn't listen. He flew close and waggled his wings at them. You know . . . friendly gesture. Well, he got shot up pretty badly."

Boyington shook his head in disgust.

"What's he doing now?"

"That's the problem, Greg. He's badgering the supply people into rearming his bird. He wants to go back for revenge."

"What? With a shot-up bird? How bad off is his plane?"

"Not bad enough to keep him out of the air," T.J. said.

"His temper is enough to do that. Where is he now?"

"In the Sheep Pen, threatening to beat up the supply men if they don't do what he says."

"I was hoping it would be quiet the rest of the day," Boyington said as he trudged off to find his exec.

chapter
14

WHEN BOYINGTON REACHED the Sheep Pen, he found most of his men had beaten him there. Without bothering to get out of their flight suits, they stood around the bar, opening beers, pouring glasses of whiskey and dispensing ice. The radio was playing the latest Dorsey record, and one man had already fallen asleep with his feet up on a table.

George Baumann was a short man with broad shoulders and a bit of a swagger. He was a capable fighter, but not as good as he thought, something which caused him no end of problems on Vella La Cava. On his first day with the squadron, he tried to take on Andy Micklin and spent the rest of the day unconscious behind the mechanics' shed. A week later he took a swing at Boyington, earning himself another nap. Baumann had calmed down some since then, but there was no telling whether or not he might try it again at any time. If it was true that he had been threatening the supply men, as T.J. reported, he was ready.

Baumann sat at a table by himself, coddling a glass of whiskey. Boyington got himself a beer from the bar, then invited himself to the table.

"George," Boyington said, putting his feet up. "I heard you had some trouble."

"Yeah . . . lousy Jap boat disguised as one of our torpedo boats," Baumann said.

"The disguise didn't fool T.J."

"Lieutenant Wylie could have been wrong," Baumann snapped.

"But he wasn't, George. That's the whole point. I want you to get out the ship recognition book and go over it again tonight."

"Oh, come on, Major. I know the book."

"Not well enough to avoid getting your ass shot off, apparently," Boyington said. "Now tell me, how bad is your plane?"

"Aw, it just took a few hits. It'll fly."

"Maybe, but not today."

"What? I'm having it refueled and rearmed. It took me half an hour to talk the supply men into doing it."

"You're not going up again today," Boyington said, taking his feet off the table and sitting up straight.

"The Jap boat that got me could be still out there," Baumann protested. "I deserve another shot at him."

"Yeah, that's right—but on another day and only after you've learned to tell American ships from Japanese ones."

Boyington finished his beer and stood up, not wanting to stay around if his presence was going to foment an argument. But Baumann was determined to have it out with him. He leaped to his feet, slamming his glass down on the table.

"I'm going after that Jap boat," he shouted, "and you're not stopping me!"

"Sit down, Baumann," Boyington said firmly.

Fuming, Baumann tried to walk past Boyington, but Pappy grabbed him by the arm.

"Where are you going?"

"To my plane!"

"You're in a bad mood, you're not prepared in the area of ship recognition, and you've been drinking. If you're going anywhere, it's to your tent, Captain."

The other Black Sheep had taken an interest in the argument, and were looking from a respectable distance.

"Let go of me!" Baumann snarled, wrenching his arm away.

"You're confined to quarters," Boyington snapped. "When you've calmed down and sobered up, I want to see you."

Baumann leaned back and threw a quick right, but Boyington sidestepped it and hit his exec with a left jab and a right to the stomach. Baumann fell to the floor, clutching his middle.

"Take him to his tent and put him to sleep," Boyington growled, walking to the bar to get himself another beer.

As two of the Black Sheep helped Baumann to his quarters, Boyington found himself a place at the bar and sipped a beer quietly until he calmed down.

"Idiot," he muttered.

A few minutes later, the men who took Baumann to his tent returned and sidled up to the bar.

"Did you put him to bed?" Boyington asked.

"Yeah, he sacked right out."

"That's funny, Greg," T.J. said. "I don't think he had that much to drink. One . . . maybe two."

"Some guys take it harder than others. Like me, for example. Tonight I intend to drown myself in beer."

"How come, Pappy?" T.J. asked.

"I thought it was gonna be a quiet afternoon, that's how come," Boyington said, fetching himself another beer and snapping off the top.

Things in the Sheep Pen seemed to be returning to normal. A poker game broke out which rivaled the radio in volume, and the bar ran out of ice, starting a huge argument over whose fault it was. Boyington had just started to enjoy himself when there could be heard the sound of a Corsair engine firing up.

"Who's that?" Boyington asked.

"Probably Micklin tinkering with an engine," Bragg said.

"What time is it now?"

"Two."

"That's in the middle of Andy's siesta," Boyington said. Then, getting a horrible thought, he jumped to his feet. "How many drinks did you say Baumann had, T.J.?"

"One . . . maybe two."

"He's suckered us!" Boyington shouted, tossing his beer aside and running from the building.

In the distance, he could see Baumann's Corsair taxiing towards the end of the runway. Shouting, Boyington ran after him, and the rest of the squadron wasn't far behind.

Baumann was already speeding down the runway by the time Boyington got to the edge of the strip. Boyington waved frantically at him, but Baumann ignored him.

"Damn," Boyington swore, and ran off to get his own plane.

Micklin was leaning on the Corsair when Boyington, out of breath and struggling to refasten his flight suit, reached it.

"How'd Baumann get that plane?"

"Beats me," Micklin said. "I was restin' at the time."

"That's great," Boyington muttered. "That's just great."

"And I'll tell you what's even better, Boyington," Micklin said. "That college boy's flying a plane with no bullets."

"What? He told me he talked the supply men into rearming her!"

"He did, but I had a talk with them about that. Like I told you a thousand times, no plane goes outta here unless I see it first. Yours is okay."

Boyington clambered into his plane and soon was roaring down the runway and up into the sky. As soon as he was above the treetops, Boyington banked to starboard and headed at full throttle towards Kolombangara. The low, swampy island was but ten miles from Vella La Cava. The Japanese on it were mainly infantry, with little antiaircraft or other major capability. So the island was largely bypassed in the drive through Vella La Cava toward Bougainville. Allied ships and pilots stayed away from it, and when the Japanese began to evacuate their troops the allies sent only a few squadrons to strafe the boats. So unimportant was the island considered, that no one bothered to send patrols ashore to make sure all the Japanese were out, and some stragglers stayed to the end of the war, living off the land.

But the enemy did send an occasional picket boat to look for stragglers, and two of them were the boats encountered by Baumann earlier in the day.

Boyington spotted Baumann ahead of him: about three miles ahead, flying at 10,00 feet. He cranked the engine up as high as it would go and flicked on the radio.

"Baumann . . . this is Boyington. . . . Where the hell do you think you're going?"

There was no reply. Not wanting to hear whatever Boyington had to say, Baumann had switched off the radio even before he took off.

"Baumann, respond! You're flying an unarmed bird! Repeat, you're flying an unarmed bird!"

Boyington watched the Corsair ahead of him, and when there was no response, assumed the radio was off. All he could do, he realized, was overtake him, and that was far from a sure thing. The coastline of Kolombangara loomed in the distance. If the Jap boats were still there . . .

Boyington pressed his throat mike another time. "Black Sheep One to La Cava."

"La Cava, go ahead, Black Sheep One."

"Get two planes into the air and have them follow me. I'm heading straight for the northeast shore of Kolombangara, chasing Captain Baumann. He's flying an unarmed bird and has apparently shut off his radio."

"Roger, Black Sheep One . . . scrambling two planes."

Boyington fiddled with the fuel mixture, hoping against hope that it would increase his speed. Baumann had reached the island, and, to make things worse, there was a small black dot on the water that could be a boat. Boyington watched in horror as Baumann's Corsair banked to starboard and headed towards the target.

Boyington closed to within a mile as Baumann put his plane into a screaming dive and set his sights on the picket boat below. There were flashes of light as the boat opened up on the Corsair.

Smoke began to pour from the engine of Baumann's Corsair. The plane pulled out of the dive and began to climb, the smoke growing thicker all the time. "No!" Boyington yelled as flames shot out of the cowling.

The plane was still climbing when the canopy was thrown backwards, and a few seconds later, a parachute blossomed below.

"La Cava, this is Black Sheep One."

"Go ahead, Major."

"Notify Air Sea Rescue. Baumann is down about one mile northeast of Kolombangara. Have them hurry it up. These are still hostile waters."

"Will do, Pappy."

Boyington reached forward and flipped the two

gun-charging switches. Then he pushed the stick forward and went for the deck. "All right, you yellow bastards," he hissed.

The Japanese seamen had been so busy shooting down Baumann and then watching him bail out that they failed to notice Boyington coming at them from the other direction. When he opened up on the boat, his first salvo cleared the decks, blowing one of the AA guns right off. As crewmen scrambled to return fire, Boyington circled and came back on them, all six guns blazing. Diving low to the water, he filled the aft hull with holes until there was a puff of smoke and a flash of fire. Pulling up and over the boat, Boyington felt his plane vibrate as the boat's fuel tanks went up, setting off the magazine. The picket boat exploded in a small fireball, and when the fire subsided, there was almost nothing left to sink.

Boyington trudged back to the bar at the Sheep Pen, grateful for the cold beer in Casey's outstretched hand. "Thanks," he said dully, downing half of it in one gulp.

"What happened, Greg?"

"The dumb bastard went up in an unarmed bird and got himself blown out of the sky by the very picket boat he was swearing to sink."

"Is he okay?"

"I guess so. He got out okay and parachuted down. I circled him until Boyle and Anderson got there to take over for me."

"And the Jap?"

"I got him," Boyington said, finishing the beer and reaching for another.

"Good deal," Casey said.

"When I get my hands on Baumann, he'll be lucky to walk, let alone fly."

"I don't blame you. Can we get Gutterman back?"

"I don't know. He must be in New York by now."

"I'll fly there personally," Casey said. "Next to Baumann, Jim was a real prince." Casey opened himself a beer and took a long pull on it. "Hey . . . I forgot to tell you!"

"What now?" Boyington asked irritably.

"No! It's good news! In fact, I doubt you'll believe it."

"I won't."

"You got a telegram from a General Hall on Guadalcanal."

"Who's he? I never heard of him."

"General Hall is the CO of that bomber wing we escorted to Bougainville this morning. Anyway, he's so nuts about us for carrying on with his bombers when the Army pilots chickened out, he's planning to pin a Silver Star on you."

Boyington perked up. "On me? You got to be kidding?"

"No, this is for real."

"Army brass doesn't decorate Marine pilots," Boyington protested.

"This one does," Casey said.

"I'll be damned. A Silver Star. I never thought they'd give me anything but aggravation."

chapter
15

WITH THE INVASION of Bougainville imminent, Rabaul increased in importance as a target. It had to be eliminated or neutralized if the Allies were to continue their progress on the road to the Philippines and, finally, Japan. Rabaul was strategically placed on the northern tip of New Britain in the Bismarck Archipelago. It had a natural harbor partially surrounded by mountains, and a number of airfields well stocked with men and equipment.

Across the narrow St. George's Channel, New Ireland acted as an outpost for fighter squadrons and spotters. In order to get to Rabaul, air assaults from the direction of the Solomons had to run an obstacle course of formidable proportions. But it was something that had to be done. Bougainville had to be taken if the Solomons were to be secured, and this couldn't be done without at least lessening the enemy's ability to make war from Rabaul.

The Black Sheep took off at dawn one day, made a rendezvous with a flight of Army B–25's, then cut across the northern part of the Solomon Sea on their way to Rabaul. Attacking Rabaul was like attacking Tokyo. It was heavily defended, with many fighters and so much antiaircraft fire one could nearly walk across the sky on top of it. Against so much force, teamwork was of paramount importance.

There could be no freewheeling dogfights like those that had taken place in the Slot. No prolonged, individual battles like the ones Boyington had had with Harachi. Attacking Rabaul was all business. On that day's mission, the two squadrons flew low over the Solomon Sea, and instead of flying up St. George's Channel with its heavy volume of military traffic, went straight inland. They kept low to the treetops as they crossed the spine of mountains running the length of New Britain, and then, after a slight jog to the north, came down on Rabaul from the land side. It was a clear day, and the base could be seen in all of its detail.

Boyington and the Black Sheep visited Rabaul often. Twice before, they had used the land approach, and both times they had caught the enemy looking out to sea. The third time they weren't so lucky. The Japs had a six-fighter lookout flying at 25,000 feet, and they spotted the attacking squadrons right away. After an hour of enforced silence, the radio suddenly came to life.

"Black Sheep One, this is Little Beaver."

"Go ahead, Little Beaver," Boyington answered.

"The cat's out of the bag, Major."

"It does look that way."

"Let's make this as fast as possible."

"Roger, Little Beaver . . . straight down the slope at treetop level. You have your target and we'll try to keep them off you."

The Black Sheep moved into attack formation around the squadron of bombers, and the mass of planes went screaming down on the Japanese base. The target of the day was the complex of sub pens and repair facilities on the Rabaul waterfront. Strangling enemy submarine capability meant not only making life a lot easier for the United States Navy, but also the journey of the regular supply ship to Vella La Cava somewhat more assured.

Once the primary target was hit, both fighters and bombers would be free to hit whatever else they could in the harbor on the way out. That could be considerable. Half a dozen destroyers, a heavy cruiser and a plethora of small craft were moored at Rabaul or steaming in or out of the harbor.

Clinging tightly to the formation of bombers, the Corsairs fended off two attacks by the Zeros already in the air. Flak sailed around Boyington's canopy like flies around a picnic. The tiny pieces of metal beat against the fuselage and made hairline cracks in the windshield. "Thank God the plane's armored," Boyington thought to himself. A Zero could never have stood it. In fact, the enemy fighters fell back rather than risk flying through the antiaircraft fire of their countrymen.

The bombers dropped their loads at a dangerously low level, and had barely gotten out of the way when the bombs struck home. One Japanese submarine took a direct hit at dockside and blew up; another was severely damaged. When the American planes pulled up and roared across the surface of the harbor at wavetop level, the sub facilities were burning fiercely.

"Okay, Black Sheep," the bomber pilot radioed. "Let's see what we can pick up on the way out."

They continued north across Rabaul harbor, making it impossible for the shore batteries and antiaircraft weapons to open up. The latter couldn't fire at the departing planes with any accuracy and without endangering their own ships. The Zeros were again pursuing, and there were another twenty that had managed to get off the ground during the American attack. But they were far behind.

Of all the naval targets he could get a shot at, Boyington picked out a Japanese destroyer. Destroyers were the biggest warships the enemy sent into the waters around Vella La Cava, and they were a major threat to the impending invasion of Bougainville. Boyington poured a long burst of .50–inch shells into the ship before passing overhead at high speed. Bragg nailed her also, and other Black Sheep pilots poured fire into another destroyer and a large inter-island transport ship.

Then the entire squadron climbed up and away from Rabaul, making a quick hop over the narrowest part of New Ireland before turning east and heading home. The flight home was without incident, which was peculiar in view of the fact that the enemy was known to have moved 100 new fighters into Bougainville in recent weeks. The two squadrons had to skirt Bougainville on their way back to the Slot, but did so without attracting a single Zero.

The Marine and Army pilots parted company off Vella La Cava.

"Little Beaver to Black Sheep One."

"Go ahead, this is Black Sheep One."

"Thanks, Pappy. We owe you guys a beer."

Boyington grinned. "The Sheep Pen's open twenty-four hours a day. If you can dump that barn door you're flying into our strip, come on!"

"I might get it in," the bomber pilot laughed, "but I'd never get it out."

"Well then," Boyington replied, "you can pick up the tab at the 'canal' some day."

"Will do, and so long."

With that, the B–52's continued on their way to Guadalcanal, while the Corsairs banked to starboard, making an easy landing on the La Cava strip.

When he had taxied to a halt and cut the engine, Boyington hopped out of the cockpit and was met on the ground by Andy Micklin. The big engineer eyed the Corsair suspiciously.

"What's the matter, Andy?"

"Where are the holes?" he asked.

"Holes?"

"Bullet holes, like you always come back with."

"No holes today," Boyington said proudly.

"I don't believe it. I just don't believe it. That's two missions in a row."

"When you're hot . . . you're hot."

"There's *nothing* wrong with this bird?" Micklin asked.

"It could stand a new canopy. We ran into pretty heavy flak."

"Canopies I don't care about," Micklin said. "They come in one piece and don't give you any trouble. Holes I care about. You just make sure you stay lucky."

"Whatever you say, Sergeant," Boyington replied, turning and walking to the Sheep Pen.

When Boyington stepped into the Sheep Pen, he found several of his men sitting around one of the larger tables, talking to an Army Intelligence officer. He was a young captain, and looked eager to please as he took notes on what the men were telling him. Boyington went to the bar and poured himself a scotch. George Baumann was there, wearing fatigues and nursing a beer.

"How was the Rendova run today?" Boyington asked, standing with his back to the bar so he could watch the Army officer.

"Fine," Baumann said. "We ran into your friend Harachi on the way out. He was making a run up and down the middle of the Slot."

"Those days will be over soon. Once Bougainville's ours, we'll be able to take it easy over the Slot at last."

"I guess so. Anyway, Harachi asked for you."

"He would. What'd he say."

Baumann imitated Harachi's broken English. " 'Boyington . . . that you, Boyington?' "

"What'd you tell him?"

"That you were in Tokyo strafing the Imperial Palace. He laughed."

"It's nice to have an enemy with a sense of humor," Boyington said.

He also felt it was nice to have Baumann in the fold at last. In the two weeks since the Kolombangara incident, Baumann had tried hard to get along with everyone. There had been no fights, not even an argument. He was a bit ill-at-ease, and Boyington still wouldn't let him fly a mission over Kolombangara again, but all in all, matters had improved so much that his mutiny was all but forgotten.

"What does that bozo want now?" Boyington asked, indicating the Army captain.

"He's compiling statistics on our recent missions. Now he wants to find out how we do it."

"Not another one," Boyington groaned.

"You've had these guys before?" Baumann asked.

"Not from the Army . . . but the Navy, the Australian Navy, and God knows the Marines have all sent 'round officers who were supposed to find out how we do it."

"Did you tell them?"

"I revealed my secret," Boyington said, holding his glass aloft and waving it around, "but they never believed me. I wonder if this one will be any different."

He sidled over to the table to find out.

chapter
16

"CAPTAIN?" BOYINGTON SAID, helping himself to a seat.

Surprised, the Army man started to get up.

"Major! I didn't see you! I . . ."

"Take it easy, would you? Being saluted makes me nervous."

"Unh . . . yes, sir," the man said, sitting back down. "Captain Baumann said it would be okay for me to ask your men a few more questions."

"Sure. Why not? You want to know how we do it, right?"

"Yes, I do. I guess you get asked that a lot."

"Now and then. I'll tell you, Nichols . . . it's teamwork."

"Teamwork?"

"Oh, I realize we don't look much like a team," Boyington laughed.

"I did notice the kangaroo," Nichols said cautiously.

"The what?"

"The kangaroo that Lieutenant Boyle got from Australia. He told me all about it."

"He did, huh? I'm glad he told someone."

"He said it arrived while you were on this morning's mission."

"Great," Boyington said sarcastically. "A kangaroo. What the hell do you feed a kangaroo? Never mind . . . it's Boyle's problem. Anyway, Captain, we're all buddies here, and that's important. Nobody flies with this outfit who doesn't fit in. That's why we work so well together when we go on a mission."

"May I ask how today's mission went?"

"I was goose-egged, but a couple of the boys scored. Jeb Pruitt—one of the new men—got one. His second, I think. Today we were escorting bombers, so I stayed close to the formation and directed the fighter defense."

"I see," Nichols replied.

"On days like this you can't go far afield," Boyington explained. "There are always other missions. Yesterday I bagged two Zeros on a patrol past Bealle."

"Yesterday?"

"That's right."

He consulted some figures he'd written in his notebook, then looked up in awe.

"That gives you twenty-two kills," Nichols said. "Sir . . . you're within three victories of Major Cannon!"

"I am?" Boyington asked disinterestedly. "I didn't know that, son."

"Did you know you're the leading Marine Corps ace?" Nichols asked.

Boyington shrugged. "I'm thirsty," he said, and asked Casey to bring him another drink.

When Casey disappeared, Pruitt and French moved in, and French took the vacant seat.

"Congratulations, Pappy," French said. "If you catch Cannon, maybe General Hall will get around to giving you that Silver Star he promised."

"You deserve one, Greg," Pruitt added. "After all . . . Major Layton got one."

"Layton shot down Admiral Shigota," Boyington

said, turning his attention and the topic of conversation away from himself. "Jeb got his second today, Nichols. Why don't you ask him about it?"

"Yeah," French agreed. "Tell him, partner."

"It wasn't much, sir," Pruitt said in embarrassment.

Jeb Pruitt was the youngest Black Sheep. He claimed to be 19, but looked 15 and probably was. Boyington didn't press the question of age, as Pruitt was the least troublesome Black Sheep and one of the better pilots. Boyington was gratified that Pruitt was learning to be a good shot as well.

"It was enough," French said.

"Congratulations, Lieutenant," Nichols said.

"Thank you, sir."

"Where did you get him?"

"Just north of the harbor . . . as we were on our way out. A flight of three Zekes came in from the side, and this one just wandered into my sights. I think one of the bombers got a piece of him, too."

French shook his head. "You got him, Jeb, just you."

"They were firing at him too."

"Yeah, well those Army guys can't hit the . . ." French remembered he was speaking to an Army captain. "Ah . . . what I mean is, their job is to drop bombs, you know. They're good at that."

Boyington smiled, finished his drink, stood up and stretched.

"If you'll excuse me, Captain."

"Sure thing, Major Boyington."

"I'm gonna go and find out about this kangaroo you mentioned."

Boyington wandered outside, wondering where Boyle had stashed his marsupial and what he'd have to say when he found them. Halfway to Boyle's tent there was the sound of approaching engines, and Boyington looked up in time to see a pair of P–38's making a landing approach.

"Lightnings," Jeb said. "We don't get too many of those around here."

"I haven't seen many at all since the Buin mission," Boyington mused. "I wonder if it's Layton."

"Nah," French said, joining them. "Layton wasn't a bad pilot for an Army man. Those guys look lost."

Boyington asked Pruitt to run over to the radio shack and find out the identity of the visitors. He was back in a moment, out of breath and excited.

"Pappy!" he exclaimed, "you'll never guess who's in those birds."

"Pilots."

"Not just pilots . . . Major Burt Cannon!"

Cannon was the leading Air Corps ace at the time, and Boyington's chief rival. Boyington didn't think much of making a contest out of who could kill more men and consequently didn't pay a great deal of attention to the so-called rivalry. But military public relations men and the American press paid a lot of attention to it, and had already made the race between Cannon and Boyington into a more spectacular show than Babe Ruth's drive for 60 home runs had been.

As Boyington tried to figure out what Cannon could be doing on Vella La Cava, the rest of the Black Sheep joined him in watching the landing. Even Boyle showed up, and in the excitement of the moment Boyington failed to notice he had a small kangaroo on a leash.

"Five bucks they show off . . . try a roll or something," Boyle said.

"Are you kidding?" French replied, "Army birdmen only know how to roll in and out of the sack."

Captain Nichols glared at French, who realized too late that he'd done it again.

"I don't know, guys," Casey said. "Look at how tight they're holding."

Indeed, Cannon and his wingman were flying wing-to-wing in perfect unison. They couldn't have done it better if they had been glued together. Cannon was an athletic man, good looking in a rough way and inclined to flash a quick smile at the drop of a hat. But his blue eyes were piercing, hawklike. They contributed to making his wingman uneasy. Lieutenant Tommy Bishop was nearly as young as Jeb Pruitt, and much in awe of the twenty-five kill flags stuck to the side of Cannon's cockpit.

"Still with me, kid?" Cannon radioed.

"Right with you, sir," the young pilot replied.

Moving as one, the two P–38's roared over the landing strip.

"Are we gonna put on a show?" Bishop asked.

"Shows are for kids just out of flight school," Cannon snarled.

"Yes, sir," Bishop said, humiliated.

"I want us to circle this field once, wing-to-wing, and land together. Nothing fancy . . . just plain good flying."

"Of course, sir."

The Lightnings made a complete turn without breaking formation and touched down lightly on the Vella La Cava airstrip. Boyington was impressed. There was nothing showy about it. As Cannon wanted it to be, the display was just good flying.

It gave Boyington all the more reason to wonder what the devil Cannon was doing at La Cava. As he tried, unsuccessfully, to come up with the answer, he finally noticed Boyle and his new pet.

"Boyle," he said in exasperation, "what the hell do you want a kangaroo for?"

"His name's Rock," Boyle said proudly. "I'm

teachin' him how to box. We can make a lot of money with this critter."

Boyington shook his head, but was unable to keep from smiling.

chapter
17

When Cannon jumped down from his P-38, he was wearing a Fifty Mission cap and a .45 automatic in an auspicious shoulder holster. Bishop wore a regulation flight suit and bore a look of reverence for his commanding officer.

Boyington pushed his way to the head of the Black Sheep clustered around the two Air Corps men.

"Boyington?" Cannon asked with one of his quick smiles.

"Greg." Boyington extended his hand, and the two aces shook heartily.

"Burt . . . and this is my wingman." Cannon waved a hand casually at his young associate. "What'd you say your name was, kid?"

The Black Sheep laughed. It seemed like a good joke, not knowing the name of one's wingman.

"Tommy," Bishop said eagerly, "Tommy Bishop."

Captain Nichols pushed to the front of the crowd.

"Major Cannon?"

"Yeah?"

"I'm Captain Nichols, Army Intelligence, stationed at Guadalcanal."

"Nichols? Oh, yeah . . . I been reading your reports on the Black Sheep." He turned to Boyington. "Are you paying him or are you really that good?"

"What do you think?" Boyington asked.

Cannon surveyed the Black Sheep, and cast an especially suspicious glance at Boyle and his kangaroo.

"You're paying him," he said.

They all broke up at that, especially Captain Nichols.

"Come on," Boyington said, "I'm buying."

As the group walked down the flight line, mechanics, mud marines and orderlies jockeyed for a sight of the famous Air Corps ace together with his main rival for the first time. It was the most exciting thing to have hit the island for some time, as if the circus had come to town.

"I'm sorry about dropping in unannounced," Cannon said. "I'm not permitted to call ahead. Washington's orders. The brass is afraid the Japanese might be monitoring our channels and make a big thing out of getting me."

Boyington was quite taken aback by that. He wanted to like Cannon, but that remark was the second piece of evidence that the Army ace was a first class hotshot, out for glory and willing to stop at nothing to get it. The first thing Boyington had noticed was the array of 25 kill flags on the side of Cannon's P-38. Kill flags were put on only for publicity photos, then taken right off. Up in the sky surrounded by Zeros, it was not considered a good idea to advertise how many Japanese pilots you'd shot down.

"How was your mission today?" Cannon asked.

"Not bad," Boyington replied. "Those boys in the 25's plastered the harbor and nobody bought the farm."

"How'd you do?"

"What do you mean?" Boyington asked.

Cannon looked a bit confused. To him, the question was perfectly clear.

"Did you get any kills?" he asked.

"Oh. No, I was too busy running the fighter defense. Some of my boys scored, though, and I got two yesterday on patrol."

"Those two give him a total of twenty-two, Major," Nichols said.

"Twenty-two," Cannon said, tossing over the meaning of that development in his mind. "That's great." He forced a smile.

"How about you, Burt?" Boyington asked.

"My last was last week . . . over Papua. Bishop and I caught a Jap patrol and bagged two of them."

"Each?"

"No. I got the both of them." Cannon looked around at the collection of tents, hastily constructed buildings and aircraft that made up the Black Sheep camp. "Nice place you got here."

"It isn't the Ritz," Boyington said. "But we've learned to love it. The one thing we've got is the best Officers' Club in the Solomons."

"Yeah?" Cannon said, interested.

"It may not be the fanciest, but it *is* the cheapest."

"What sort of stuff do you stock?"

"Are you a drinking man, Burt?" Boyington asked.

"I guess you could say that."

"Then you came to the right place. We've got your standard issue brandy and medicinal alchohol, of course. But we do a lot of horse trading with the Navy guys on the other side of the island, and we also pick up a lot of things in 'Canal. Today we can offer you scotch, bourbon and two kinds of beer. We've been trying to get some gin from Australia so we can make use of all the lime trees on this rock, but the last man I sent to Australia came home with a kangaroo instead."

"You sure do have unique problems, Greg," Cannon laughed.

The men piled into the Sheep Pen and clustered around the bar as Casey played bartender long enough to supply everyone. Both Boyington and Cannon ordered beers, and to the immense approval of all in the room, clinked their bottles together.

"To the Black Sheep," Cannon toasted, "the hottest squadron in the Pacific."

A great cheer went up which became even more vivid when Cannon finished his toast by clapping an arm around Capt. Nichols and saying, "Even if it did take a little help from the Air Corps."

For a time, Boyington was warming up to Cannon. He'd started to forget the kill flags, the shoulder-holstered .45, the Fifty Missions cap and even the remark as to how the whole Jap military was out to get him. Then Cannon took Boyington aside, and in a friendly tone said, "It's going to be great flying with you guys."

Boyington nearly bit the top off the bottle.

"What?" he exclaimed.

Cannon took an envelope out of his pocket and handed it over.

Boyington glanced at the papers inside it long enough to realize what they were, and then headed for the door. "Let's go some place we can talk," he said.

Cannon shrugged and followed Boyington out to the side of the Sheep Pen, then plunked himself down atop a rusting oil barrel while Boyington read the orders. Cannon finished his beer, then started playing with his .45—checking the slide, swinging it around and sighting it on various points around the base.

"I never heard of orders like these," Boyington spat.

"This is the first time it's ever been done. Look, I wouldn't blame you if you got so smoked, you kicked my butt outta here. If I was in your place, that's what I would do."

"I still may."

Cannon laughed as if to dismiss the thought, but

continued sighting down the barrel of his automatic. He looked like a man very eager to shoot something.

"The Air Corps wants me to run up a score," he said. "So they cut those orders to attach myself to your squadron."

"That's not what they say," Boyington protested. "They say you can float . . . attach yourself to any squadron in the South Pacific. Why did you pick us?"

After thinking a moment, Cannon re-holstered his gun and sat down next to Boyington.

"Greg," he said, "I'm a guy just like you, out here trying to do a job. Maybe part of that job has some propaganda overtones, but it's still my job. I've been reading our reports on the Black Sheep's performance, especially in your recent Rabaul raids. You guys are hot! Knocking 'em out of the sky right and left. What can it hurt if I get a little of that?"

"A lot!" Boyington snapped. "The Black Sheep are a team, a smooth running team. In fact, we're the Yankees' starting lineup! We work together like a machine, and I won't jeopardize that so you can run up a score!"

"You don't have to," Cannon said. "I'll play team ball, and you're the captain."

Boyington sighed. There didn't seem to be anything he could do about it.

"Let me stick around a few days," Cannon said, pressing home his case. "Let me take a shot at what I can get and I'll be on my way. Whattya say, Greg?"

"I say according to these orders I don't have a choice."

"Hey! That's not the way I want it to be," Cannon said. "I'll play team ball. I swear it."

"Raiding Rabaul isn't like mixing it up one-for-one over the Slot . . . or even like a dogfight over Papua. It's like attacking a goddam fortress . . . or flying up the muzzle of a flak gun. The only way to do it is to stick to precision team playing. I could have run up a score today if I didn't mind letting the B–25's get shot to hell. But I didn't do it."

Boyington stared at Cannon for a long time, trying to figure out the Air Corps ace. Was he sincerely doing his best to win the war, or merely looking for a place in history? Boyington couldn't be sure, and decided to withhold judgment.

"Okay," he sighed, "maybe I am coming down on you too hard. We got a low-level sweep in the morning. We brief in the Sheep Pen a half-hour before take-off."

"Aye-aye, sir," Cannon said with a quick grin that made Boyington squirm.

chapter
18

As USUAL Boyington's white bull terrier, Meatball, was fighting him for possession of the cot. It was nearly two in the morning, and the racket in camp was tremendous. Neither Washing Machine Charlie nor a strafing run by Harachi's squadron could have made the noise the Black Sheep kicked up in the Sheep Pen. Half asleep and grumbling, Boyington shoved the dog a few inches to one side and pulled a pillow over his head. It shut out some of the noise, and he went back to his dream.

The Sheep Pen was packed to the rafters. Every officer on the base except Boyington was there, as well as most of the nurses. Major Cannon sat at Jerry Bragg's old organ, playing a flying song and trying to get the Black Sheep to sing along with him. Over by the bar, Boyle had chalked a large circle on the floor and was kneeling inside it, trying to get his kangaroo to box with him. A dozen men and women crowded around the perimeter of the circle, egging the animal on, but to no avail.

The radio blared on in spite of Cannon, and everywhere were bottles of a particularly good scotch, far better than the kind usually served in the Sheep Pen. Outside the door, noncoms and enlisted men peered inside, unable to enter the Officers Club, but still provided with bottles of the excellent scotch. In all, it was a drunken bash of greater dimensions than any seen in Vella La Cava for some time.

Cannon had grown tired of the flying song and switched to "The Battle Hymn of the Republic," which he sang in a drunken baritone. Don French leaned heavily on his shoulders, singing the chorus and conducting an imaginary orchestra with one hand.

"Don't crash on me, Don," Cannon said.

"No, sir," French replied, and promptly collapsed. He caromed off the bass keys of the organ and landed on his back, where he stayed.

"He forgot to lower his landing gear," Bragg shouted. Laughing, he stumbled away from Cannon and toward the people clustered around Boyle and his kangaroo. "Give him hell, Rock," Bragg shouted again, weaving drunkenly into the chalk circle with the two combatants.

"Get out, Jerry!" Boyle snapped. "This is a private fight!"

"It doesn't look like much of a fight at all. Why don't you teach that thing to pick daisies?"

"You're gonna be pushin' up daisies if you don't beat it," Boyle said.

Boyle tried again to get Rock to spar with him. "Come on, Rock," he said, "you can do it. Put up your dukes." It was to no avail. The kangaroo sat back on its tail and occasionally gave a little poke with its paws, but it looked nothing like boxing. Finally, Boyle stood and threw his hands up.

"It's no use," he said angrily. "He just isn't a fighter. I'm gonna have to trade him in for a wallaby."

Bragg stepped forward and pushed Boyle out of the way. "You got to give him an example," he said.

"What?"

"You got to show him how to throw a punch."

"Show him how, huh?" Boyle said. "Okay."

Boyle cold-cocked Bragg with a strong right,

knocking him over a table. The table cracked and fell apart, and chairs were scattered to either side. A huge cheer rose from the crowd. Boyle gave a whoop of delight. He picked up a half-filled bottle, drained it, then hurled the empty through a window.

The noise woke up Boyington. He sat bolt upright. "What the hell's going on?" he growled.

Boyington got up, pulled on his pants, and, while the dog took the opportunity to occupy the entire cot, stalked angrily out of his tent and over to the Sheep Pen.

In front of the building, T.J. was stretched out on the hood of a jeep, one arm around a pretty brunette nurse and the other holding a bottle of the good scotch. T.J. was quite drunk, and struggling with the decision of which to take advantage of first—the good scotch or the woman. He saw Boyington through bleary eyes.

"Ten-hut," he said, without enthusiasm.

"At ease," Boyington said dryly. "And tell me . . . what's going on?"

"Major Cannon is throwing a party, Greg." He held up the bottle for Boyington to try. "Those Lightnings are beautiful. The tail booms hold two cases of scotch each."

Boyington took the bottle from T. J. and tested it. It wasn't bad; good, in fact.

"Cannon brought eight cases of this?"

"Yep," T.J. replied.

Carrying the bottle with him, Boyington pushed through the crowd around the Sheep Pen and went inside.

French and Bragg were still out cold, and Boyle was crawling around on his hands and knees trying to find Rock. The kangaroo had taken off when Boyle tossed the bottle through the window, and was nowhere to be found. Cannon had given up trying to play the organ and was sitting with his back to it, using it to prop himself up.

Samantha Brown, Boyington's favorite nurse, stood alone by the bar, watching the proceedings with faint amusement. She was a beautiful girl, with long blond hair. None of the men tried to hit on her. Having an illegal party was one thing; flirting with the CO's girl quite another. Boyington went to her and gave her a little kiss.

"I hope you're not flying in the morning," Samantha said.

Boyington frowned, then banged on the bar with the bottle he carried. "I thought I closed this bar two hours ago," he yelled.

There were a lot of groans, and much yelling.

"Come on, Pappy," Jeb protested. He was drunker than he'd ever been in his young life.

"The bar's closed!" Boyington insisted.

The complaining continued as the Sheep Pen cleared out. Bragg and French were carried out, and Boyle found Rock behind the bar and tried to drag him out. Cannon left his seat and weaved over to Boyington.

"My apologies, Major," he said drunkenly. "It's my fault. However, I will be ready to fly at dawn's early light."

"Uh huh."

Cannon offered a sloppy salute, then was helped out of the Sheep Pen by his wingman. When he was gone, Samantha took Boyington by the arm.

"Something bothers me about him, Greg," she said.

"Oh, I don't know," Boyington replied. "He might drink a bit too much."

Samantha looked at Boyington quizzically. He broke out laughing, and hugged her. "This is good scotch," he said, "and I *did* ask him if he was a drinking man."

Leaning heavily on Tommy Bishop, Cannon weaved down the row of tents which made up the Black Sheep's living quarters. As the Marine pilots fumbled their way into their tents, the two Air Corps men struggled to reach the one assigned them for their stay on La Cava. When the last Black Sheep had fallen into his bunk, Cannon and Bishop paused outside their tent.

"Get some sleep," Cannon said, standing on his own. "We have to fly in a couple of hours."

"What about you, sir?" Bishop asked.

"I want to get some air, kid. There was too much smoke in that bar."

"Good night, sir."

"Good night," Cannon said, taking a deep breath and walking off, stone cold sober.

chapter
19

WHEN DAWN CAME, Andy Micklin found himself under the engine of one of the reserve Corsairs the mechanics were always struggling to put back together. This particular one had had its engine shot up by a Zero a week earlier, and Micklin was just getting around to repairing the damage. He peered into the bowels of the big radial engine, using a small wrench to disconnect an oil line.

"Stan!" he yelled.

Up in the cockpit of the Corsair, mechanic Stan Richards was lying on his back, his feet sticking over the side, his head under the front control panel. He had already replaced the fuel reserve warning light, and was trying to find out why the cylinder temperature gauge wasn't working.

"Yeah, Sarge?" he called back.

"Whatever you do," Micklin yelled, "don't hit the oil cooler pump switch!"

"Oil cooler pump . . . right, Sarge."

Richards heard only the last half of the command, and quickly flicked on the switch. A stream of oil hit Micklin smack in the face from the line he'd just disconnected. He didn't make a sound, just stood for a second, then slowly moved out from under the engine. He walked around the plane toward the cockpit, murder in his eyes.

Micklin climbed up and peered into the cockpit at Richards, who still had his head under the front panel, engrossed as he was in the wiring.

"Stan?" Micklin said softly.

"Yeah, Sarge?" Richards asked, pulling out from under the panel. He saw Micklin's oil–drenched face and was too terrified to speak.

"If I was you, Stan," Micklin said in a soft voice, "I'd disappear." He raised his voice to a roar. *"Until the next war!"*

"On my way, Sarge," Richards said, trying to scramble out of the cockpit.

"Get back in there, you idiot!" Micklin yelled, pushing him back in.

"Whatever you say, Sarge."

Richards ducked back under the front panel, grateful to be alive. Micklin wiped the oil off his face with a rag and looked down the long line of parked fighter planes. Down towards the end, he thought he saw something move in one of the cockpits. It couldn't have been one of the Black Sheep; they didn't get out of bed until the last possible moment, and Micklin knew they'd had a big party the night before.

Major Cannon was just easing himself out of Boyington's cockpit when Micklin got to the side of the plane.

"Hey you!" he bellowed, "get outta my airplane!"

Cannon dropped to the ground in front of the big technical sergeant.

"What were you doin' up there?" Micklin growled.

"Just locking the controls," Cannon said offhandedly. "Most pilots just don't appreciate how hard it is on an airplane to leave the controls unlocked on the ground."

Micklin was impressed. "That's what I keep telling them college boys," he said. "But they got ear wax or something. You're Major Cannon, aren't you?"

"Yeah," Cannon said, extending a hand. "And you're Sergeant Micklin. I heard of you."

"Me?" Micklin said, shaking Cannon's hand.

"Word gets around."

Micklin was astounded at the suggestion that his fame as a mechanic was growing. To him, he'd always been known as the tough–ass, old–line Marine sergeant who'd knock the teeth out of any officer who gave him a hard time. And all officers seemed determined to give him a hard time.

But here was a hotshot Air Corps major—a quadruple ace with more kills than even Boyington—who'd heard of him because of the way he did his job. Micklin pulled out a pack of matches and was about to light his cigar stub when he remembered the oil.

He looked at the stub. It was covered with oil. Micklin scowled and tossed it into the dirt. It was replaced immediately by Cannon, who pulled an expensive corona out of his pocket and handed it to Micklin.

"Thanks, Major," Micklin said as Cannon lit the cigar for him. "This is the best cigar I've had since I got shipped out."

"Come with me, Sarge," said Cannon. "There's something I'd like to show you."

As Micklin puffed happily on his new cigar, he let Cannon put an arm around his shoulders and lead him away from the Corsairs toward where the two Lightnings were tied down.

"You know," Cannon said, "you're one of the reasons I came to La Cava."

"I am?"

"From what I've heard there's not an Air Corps mechanic worth lighting your cigar. None of the ones who've worked on my bird have been any good, that's for sure. The kids I get as mechanics might be able to soup up a jeep, but when it comes to a P–38 . . ." Cannon shook his head sadly. "They ain't got it."

"Is that a fact?" Micklin said, surprised to hear such an admission from an Army man. He had suspected as much himself.

"It's gospel, Sarge," Cannon said, stopping in front of his Lightning.

"She sure is a sweet–lookin' bird," Micklin said, admiring the P–38.

"She'd be even sweeter if you'd tune her up for me."

"I dunno, Major . . ."

"I keep getting sand in the superchargers. Sand and coral dust from these damn islands. I know I got no right to ask, but if you could see your way clear to spend a little time on her, I'd sure appreciate it."

"The problem is," Micklin said, "I got to do a lot of work on the Corsairs. That one I was workin' on was shot to hell last week over Rendova, and there's two more in pretty bad shape. You see, Boyington's got this Colonel Lard on his back all the time. If Boyington don't put up a full squadron of fifteen planes, Lard will break up the Black Sheep. So . . ."

"This really won't take long," Cannon said. "I just need you to look at the superchargers and maybe listen to the right engine a bit. I think there's something wrong with the mixture."

Micklin thought a minute, then shrugged. "What the hell," he said. "I'll do it. It might be interesting."

"Good," Cannon said enthusiastically. "Anything you need I'll have flown in within twenty-four hours. Anything."

"Anything?" Micklin asked.

"Name it."

"A box of these cigars?"

Cannon went to the access panel on the starboard boom and pulled it open.

"That request might take . . . oh, ten seconds," Cannon said, handing Micklin a box of cigars.

The sergeant stared at the box a moment, then grinned and took them.

"That's what's been missing around here," he said, "a little inter–service cooperation."

Jerry Bragg dreamt that a large, furry creature was eating his arm. It was the most realistic dream he'd had since joining the Marines. He woke up with a shriek to discover it was reasonably true. Boyle's kangaroo was nibbling on his skivvies. Bragg shrieked again and jumped out of bed. The frightened kangaroo jumped backward, knocking over Boyle's cot. Still yelling, Boyle clambered to his feet and tried to clear the fog from his eyes. The kangaroo bolted for the door, pushed aside the mosquito netting and was gone.

Bragg got a good look at Boyle and suddenly remembered how he happened to go to sleep the night before. "You cold-cocked me, you bastard!" he yelled. He swung at Boyle but missed and fell onto the floor.

Boyle paid no attention. The kangaroo was gone. He looked everywhere, then thought of the door. Boyle ran out of the door screaming the name of his kangaroo. Rock was nowhere to be found. Boyle was set to run into the jungle after the animal when Boyington caught him and tossed him back into his tent.

"Get dressed, you bum," Boyington snapped. "We fly in half an hour."

Boyington went to the Sheep Pen and ate a quick breakfast of rubber pancakes, burned eggs and coffee. Then he laid out the maps for the morning briefing.

One by one, the Black Sheep dragged themselves in. Looking like an outfit that had been in battle ten days straight, they ate breakfast by rote, then gathered around Boyington for the briefing. They looked asleep on their feet.

Boyington took a deep breath and faced them. "The recon photos taken after yesterday's raid on

Rabaul," he said, "showed that the bombers nailed two subs and severely damaged the dockside facilities." At this information, a very weak cheer went up from the men. "Now, we're being asked to switch our attention to the destroyers based in Rabaul. As you know, they ran the Slot the other day and shelled every beachhead we've got on New Georgia. The Army can't mount another bombing raid for at least twenty-four hours, so we're being ordered to make a low–level sweep into Rabaul harbor."

"That's wonderful," Bragg said dully, rubbing the side of his head.

"We'll come in from the sea this time," continued Boyington. "The last three times we've paid a call on that harbor, we've taken the land approach—over the mountains and down. This time they'll be waiting. So we'll swing north of New Ireland, cut south across that island at its narrowest point, and fly sea level straight into Rabaul. I figure if we surprise 'em, we can get two runs in before they have a chance to get enough Zeros up to do us harm."

There were a few grunts and one moan, but no questions. Boyington continued. "I'll lead A–flight. Casey will lead B–flight. We're going strictly for the destroyers. Micklin's heavied our loads with armor–piercing ammo, but if you go after anything bigger than a destroyer, you'll only dent it." Boyington looked at French, who seemed to be asleep. "Repeat that, Don," he said.

French opened one eye and glared at his boss. "'Micklin's heavied our loads with armor–piercing ammo, but if you go after anything bigger than a destroyer, you'll only dent it. Repeat that, Don'."

"One of these days," Boyington said, shaking a fist, "one of these days."

"But not today," French said with a smile.

"Okay, Major Cannon will fly top cover on this

one. That's just in case some Zekes happen to be above us. Is that okay with you, Major?"

"Anything you say, Greg," Cannon grinned.

"Mount up. And grab some oxygen before you take off. It'll help sober you up."

The Black Sheep got up and went for their planes with a discernible lack of enthusiasm. Only Jeb Pruitt had the strength to run toward his Corsair. Bragg watched him with a pained expression.

"Did you guys ever notice how loud Jeb runs?" he asked.

Boyle nodded. "The first one to backfire an engine is going to catch it," he said.

"That's right!" Casey agreed in horror. "We got to start up those loud engines!"

"Don't feel bad," French said. "How'd you like to be Major Cannon? He's gotta start two engines."

But Cannon wasn't hung over, as he had not gotten drunk. Both Boyington and he climbed into their respective cockpits, feeling fresh and eager. The rest of the Black Sheep went right for the oxygen, hoping it would clear their heads.

"We gotta do it sooner or later," Boyington said, touching the starter. "Hold on to your heads."

chapter
20

THE CORSAIRS FLEW at 20,000 feet on a course which took them north–northeast to the strait lying between Bougainville and Choiseul. That was the course flown by the squadron as the first leg of a typical patrol. But instead of cutting east to skirt the southern coast of Choiseul as on a typical patrol, the planes dropped to the deck and flew at sea level through the straits. They continued on a north–northeasterly course until well north of Choiseul, then cut west to circle Bougainville, heading for New Ireland.

Boyington led the flight as it banked south to cut across that narrow island. Rabaul harbor lay ahead, filled with ships and bristling with guns. The ruse had worked. Bougainville radar was fooled into thinking the Black Sheep were on a routine patrol past Choiseul, and Rabaul fighter defense was fooled into expecting a fourth assault from the land side. Boyington pressed his throat mike.

"Okay, you meatheads," he radioed, "I think we weren't expected. Remember—one pass on the deck, climb and circle, and one diving attack. Go for the destroyers only, and concentrate on anything that looks breakable. We want to keep those guys in the repair docks for some time."

The invasion of Bougainville was imminent, and

the more enemy ships disabled before it occurred, the
better.

"Major Cannon and Lieutenant Bishop—climb to
angels 20 and cover us. And if there's anything you can
pick off up there, be my guest."

"That's a deal, Greg," Cannon answered.

Boyington watched in admiration as the two
P–38's headed up toward the sky. With their twin engines, the Lightnings could climb to 20,000 feet in four
and one-half minutes, faster than either Corsairs or
Zeros. After the previous night's drunken party, Boyington had definite qualms about Cannon. Still, it felt
good to have high cover.

As Boyington had hoped, Rabaul antiaircraft was
confused at the sight of two groups of strange planes—
one group climbing and the other flying at sea level. At
first, they thought the P–38's were Japanese planes
climbing after takeoff from one of the far coastal strips.
By the time all the planes were identified as American,
antiaircraft had to be divided between two distantly
separated targets.

The Black Sheep had no trouble finding targets.
From their vantage point at sea level, the numerous
destroyers in the harbor were highly vulnerable. Boyington wanted to make a shambles of their bridges and
AA guns. If he could keep them in port making minor
repairs for another week, the Allied invasion of Bougainville could proceed without their hindrance. He
knew that the enemy would never send destroyers into
the Slot if they were inadequately protected against
Allied aircraft. The lesson of Midway, where four
Japanese carriers were destroyed by American fighter
planes, was one the enemy wasn't about to forget.

On their low–level run, the Black Sheep caught the
AA crews napping. Before they could crank their guns
down for horizontal fire, the Corsairs were pumping
half-inch shells into them. The bullets raked the de-

stroyers, igniting AA magazines and shattering bridge equipment. Boyington saw a puff of smoke followed by flame as his machine guns started a fire in the forward five-inch gun turret of a Fubuki-class destroyer before he had to break off and climb away from the shore batteries.

"Everybody okay?" he asked as the Corsairs fought for altitude and the destroyer antiaircraft gunners frantically cranked their guns back up for vertical fire.

"No problems, Pappy," Boyle answered, and the other pilots responded likewise.

The Black Sheep topped off at 10,000 feet and prepared for another dive. Beneath them, several small fires were blazing on three of the destroyers.

"This time, let's clear the decks from above, bow to stern," Boyington said.

One by one, the Corsairs dived back down toward the enemy ships. This time, the Japanese gunners were ready and threw up a wall of fire. Flak shells burst around the American fighters, and tracers made bright white arcs past their canopies as every AA gun in Rabaul harbor seemed to open up.

Don French quickly settled his sights on the open munitions hold of an old Fubuki and poured round after round into it. Before he reached the bottom of his dive, the magazine went up in a blinding flash and the destroyer shuddered, then blew apart. Steel plates flew in all directions and a cloud of black smoke obscured what remained of the target.

As French pulled out of his dive, an oil slick from the wrecked ship caught fire and lapped against the pier, setting that afire as well.

Boyington took down the radio and lookout mast of the destroyer he had picked, riddling the bridge deck as well. As quickly as they had come, the Black Sheep were pulling out of their dives and fighting once again for altitude. Just when Boyington was convinced the squadron had taken on a charmed life, there was a frantic shout over the radio.

"I'm hit," Jeb cried out as antiaircraft fire hit his plane and smoke began to pour from under the cowling.

Boyington looked quickly at the stricken Corsair.

"How bad is it, Jeb?"

Pruitt was too busy scanning the instruments to answer, as he tried to determine just what was wrong.

"Jeb?"

"It's okay," Pruitt answered. "I'm losing some fuel. The oil pressure is low. She's running smooth, though. I'll make it home."

The Corsairs leveled off at 10,000 and looked around for enemy fighters. Off in the distance, a flight of about 40 Zeros was rising from two fields west of the harbor.

"You'd better get out of here, Jeb," Boyington said.

"That looks like a good idea."

"French, you'd better go with him. The rest of us have another run to make."

"I thought you planned on two runs?" Bragg asked.

"I did, but those Zekes are far enough off to let us get in another sweep. We'll do one more like the last one and see if we can't put another dent in 'em. A weekend off for the man who gets another destroyer like Don did."

"Hey," French protested, "what about me?"

"You get a cup of black coffee," Boyington snapped. "After the show you put on last night, you don't need a weekend off."

"Black Sheep One, this is Top Cover One," Cannon radioed. "Let Don have another shot at that weekend pass. We'll take Little Brother home."

Boyington looked up at the two P–38's circling far above.

"Roger," Boyington said, "you got him, and thanks. French, join up and get ready for another run."

French radioed his acknowledgement, and the Black Sheep readied themselves for a final run at the destroyers in Rabaul harbor. As they did so, Pruitt pointed his Corsair north away from the withering AA fire, climbed to 20,000 feet and joined up with the two Lightnings. Cannon and Bishop flew behind and slightly above him.

"I sure appreciate the escort, Major," Pruitt said.

"Don't think twice about it. You're covered, son."

Pruitt smiled, relaxed a bit, and kept a watchful eye on the instruments as the three planes set a course for Vella La Cava. There were no interceptions by enemy aircraft, and by the time the American planes had flown through the channel between Bougainville and Choiseul and were back in the Slot, Pruitt felt sure they'd make it.

In the cockpits of the two Lightnings, matters were a little different. Cannon got his wingman's attention, then held up two fingers indicating for him to switch to a radio channel where they could have some privacy. Both Air Corps pilots did so.

"Bishop?" Cannon radioed.

"Here, sir."

"I don't want to alarm that kid, but that smoke his engine is putting out is gonna attract Zeros like blood attracts sharks. When we switch back to channel one, you stay off the radio. Use hand signals if you spot the enemy. Remember . . . I don't want to panic that kid into losing his plane. Let's get some altitude. When the Japs come, I want to have an edge."

"Yes, sir," Bishop answered as the Lightning powered up and climbed away from Pruitt's Corsair. The Marine pilot kept his course and altitude, unaware the Air Corps pilots had climbed above him.

Halfway across the Slot, Pruitt's Corsair gave up the ghost. There was a loud bang as the engine misfired, and the whole plane began to buck. Pruitt fought the controls until he got the plane steadied to a tolerable level.

"The cylinder head temp's in the yellow and she's starting to buck," he radioed. "The plugs must be fouling. Micklin's gonna kill me. He hates fouled plugs."

Pruitt waited for a reply, and when he didn't get one, twisted around to look for the P–38's. When he didn't see them, he got worried.

"Major Cannon? You there? Major."

There was a pause before Cannon got back to him.

"Relax, kid," Cannon replied. "We just decided to get a little altitude. We're above and behind you. Got you in sight."

"Thanks," Pruitt said, quite relieved. "She's turning into a real cocktail shaker."

"Can you still make it to La Cava?"

"If it doesn't get any worse."

Forbidden by Cannon to use the radio, Bishop looked around for enemy planes. If they were ever going to spot any, it would be then. Pruitt's airplane was leaving a smoke trail several miles long, an open invitation to Zeros. Before long, Bishop spotted two Zeros out of Bougainville flying up Pruitt's smoke trail like hungry sharks chasing a wounded fish.

Bishop signaled frantically to Cannon, who saw the enemy planes and nodded. He was not, however, about to tell Pruitt about them. Cannon intended to let Pruitt act as unwitting bait for the two Japanese planes. When they tried to get Pruitt, Cannon would get them. It was dangerous, even cruel flying; it was taking liberties with Pruitt's life.

But it had made Cannon the leading ace, a position he intended to keep.

chapter
21

"HOW'S THE OIL PRESSURE?" Cannon asked.

Pruitt fought to maintain air speed and at the same time to check the instrument readings Cannon was asking him for in an attempt to keep him occupied.

"It's still dropping slightly," he replied.

"Manifold pressure?"

"Twenty-eight."

The Zeros continued bearing down on Pruitt, who had become totally preoccupied with the readings on the instrument panel. He felt he was secure, having the Number One ace flying escort for him.

Bishop was a lot less secure. He had an idea of what Cannon was up to, but he didn't dare contradict him. Major Cannon was the boss. Bishop was privileged to be flying with him, and Cannon frequently reminded him of the fact. But as the Zeros drew closer to the unwitting Marine flyer, Bishop grew more and more nervous.

"RPM's steady or surging?" Cannon asked.

"A slight surge now and then," Pruitt replied.

The enemy planes were right on Pruitt's tail and ready to fire. Bishop could stand it no longer. Cannon or no Cannon, he had to warn Pruitt. Bishop hit the mike button.

"Pruitt! Zekes on your tail!"

As Pruitt went into a diving turn, Cannon dived on the enemy planes, his guns blazing. The first Zero flamed instantly and went down, spinning and trailing a great amount of smoke. The second enemy plane stuck to Pruitt, pouring fire into his Corsair.

"I'm hit. . . . I'm hit!" Pruitt yelled as the plane started to go down, the stream of smoke from its engine turning into a torrent.

"Jeb's going in," Bishop radioed.

Cannon paid attention neither to Pruitt nor to Bishop. His entire attention remained focused on the second Zero as he swooped down after it.

"Bail out, Jeb! Bail out!"

Cannon got the Zero where he wanted it and pressed the trigger. A long burst of shells poured into the enemy plane, blowing the canopy off and silencing the engine. Finally it blew apart, and Cannon had to climb sharply to get away from the debris.

Bishop followed Pruitt's Corsair as it slid sharply toward the ocean, praying all the time he'd be able to get out. There was no way he'd be able to ditch successfully. At the last possible moment, the canopy of the Corsair shot back and Pruitt bailed out. A white parachute fluttered briefly in the morning sun before Pruitt hit the water.

The Corsair smacked into the water a hundred yards ahead of him and exploded. Burning gas and oil covered the water as Cannon and Bishop circled above.

Cannon smiled victoriously. "This is Top Cover One calling Air-Sea Rescue," he radioed.

"Air–Sea Munda . . . go ahead Top Cover One."

"We got a splasher . . . coordinates zero–seven–one . . . alpha–niner."

"Roger . . . zero–seven–one . . . alpha–niner."

"We have enough fuel to maintain a cap for . . ." Cannon checked his fuel gauge. ". . . twenty minutes . . . over."

"We have that, Top Cover. Dumbo on his way ... ETA fifteen minutes."

With Lieutenant Bishop on his wingtip, Cannon began to make slow circles over the spot where Jeb Pruitt had splashed down.

Micklin and Richards stood by the flight line, waiting for the Lightnings to return. Micklin puffed on one of the cigars Cannon had given him and watched impatiently as Cannon and Bishop landed, then taxied slowly down the field.

"Some pretty birds, aren't they?" Micklin said between puffs.

"Yeah, Sarge."

"Not like them junk heaps we usually have to work on."

"No, Sarge."

"They have a much better cockpit layout than the Corsairs," Micklin went on.

"Right, Sarge. Most of the instruments are in front, where you don't have to hunt for them."

Having recently feared for his life as a result of the oil episode, Richards wanted to be agreeable. Even when Micklin told him they'd be working on the Lightnings instead of the Corsairs that day, he didn't object. But he was planning to ask. He was nowhere nearly as tough as Micklin, but he could run faster. The open runway seemed a convenient place to run if need be.

"Look at Boyington's plane," Micklin said. "He's got the trim tab controls under his left elbow, the radio control box under his right elbow, and the wing flap control stuck where you can never find it. The only thing that is easy to get to is the emergency CO_2 for crash landings. In Boyington's case, that's good."

Richards laughed and screwed up his courage. "Look, Sarge," he said cautiously, "are you sure it's a good idea for us to work on Cannon's plane?"

"What?"

"I mean, we're supposed to work on our own planes. Captain Baumann had to fly with only three birds this morning. When Major Boyington hears about it . . ."

"You let me worry about Boyington," Micklin snapped. "Did you bring the plug puller and gapper?"

"Yeah, Sarge."

"How much coolant?"

"Ten gallons."

Micklin adjusted his cap, and his fingers came away soaked with oil from earlier in the morning.

"Oil!" he asked angrily.

"Plenty of oil," Richards said, deciding then and there to question Micklin's orders no further.

The two mechanics walked up to Cannon as he shut down his engines and jumped from the cockpit.

"How'd it go?" Micklin asked.

Cannon held up two fingers and gave Micklin a broad grin.

"I got two!" he said proudly. "Thanks to you, that is. I swear she's ten knots faster, Sarge."

Micklin swelled with pride, and tugged proudly on his cigar while Cannon ducked under the port wing of his Lightning and walked away. Lieutenant Bishop had just jumped down from his plane and seemed dazed. He nearly walked into Micklin, who stood ready to attack the port engine of Cannon's Lightning.

"I guess you want yours looked at, too?" Micklin snarled.

Bishop was shocked into his senses, and looked up at Micklin, whom he had never met. "Oh . . . no thanks," he said.

Micklin too was shocked. Very seldom did any pilot turn down an offer to have his plane worked on.

"What's the matter with you? What happened this morning? Cannon got two Japs, he said."

"Yeah . . . he did."

"You get skunked? Is that it?"

"Jeb got flamed."

"Pruitt? The high school kid Boyington's teaching how to fly? Is he still alive?"

"I think so. Air-Sea Rescue picked him up."

"He's still alive. I know these guys. They never die. They always come back to mess up more if my planes. Why don't you go to the Sheep Pen and get drunk with the rest of the college boys?"

"I'm not a college boy," Bishop said.

"That makes you the only one."

"I flew a crop duster in Arkansas. A converted Waco-9."

Micklin was impressed. "And you're still alive? Those things run on rubber bands."

"Yeah," Bishop laughed. "They are a bit under-powered."

"Go get drunk before Boyington gets back here and drinks the island dry."

"I don't want to go to the Officers' Club," Bishop said, shuffling his feet. "I don't want to see anybody. Not until I'm sure that Jeb's okay."

"I told you," Micklin said angrily. "Black Sheep don't die. But I can see why you don't want to drink with them. I got a couple cases of beer in the mechanics' shed. Go have a couple. But if you drink it all, I'll break your neck."

"I don't drink much."

"Then you can have some of mine."

"I'll think about it, Sarge," Bishop said, "and thanks."

He ran off to catch up with Cannon, and did so just before the major got to the Sheep Pen.

"Major?"

"What?" Cannon snapped.

"Why didn't you warn Jeb that Zeros were on his tail? Why did you wait? I have to know."

Cannon stopped in his tracks and turned on the young officer. "I *told* you to maintain radio silence. I said to use *hand* signals."

"But . . ."

"If that kid is dead, it's because of you!"

Bishop looked as if he'd been slapped in the face, and he couldn't think of anything to say.

"You saw me blow that lead Zeke with one burst," Cannon went on. "I was set. All I had to do was kick right rudder . . ." He snapped his fingers. ". . . and the second one would have gone the same way. But you had to yell! The kid dove and that Zeke went after him, busting my shot! Like I said . . . if Pruitt is dead, it's because of you."

Cannon was the ace of aces. His tone was commanding, and Bishop never could stand up to him.

"I . . . I didn't know."

"Tell that to Pruitt!" Cannon snapped, turning and stalking away.

Bishop was devastated. He watched Cannon disappear into the Sheep Pen, then turned and trudged off to the mechanics' shed to drink Micklin's beer.

chapter
22

BISHOP SPENT half an hour in the mechanics' shed, drinking Micklin's beer. He had as much of it as he could stand, then trudged on toward the Sheep Pen. He didn't want to go there, but he was intent upon getting drunk, and finishing up Micklin's beer was a riskier proposition than fighting the Japanese. There was no whiskey in the tent he shared with Cannon, so he had to go to the Sheep Pen.

Cannon was there, sitting at a table with three of the nurses who frequented the Black Sheep camp; Susan Ames, Nancy Tommason and Ellie Kovaks. Cannon was all smiles, telling stories about his many battles, and immediately called Bishop over to sit with them. Drunk enough not to care, Bishop complied. The juke box was blaring a loud jitterbug number. Captain Nichols and Samantha tore up the middle of the room dancing to it. Cannon had put his Fifty Mission cap on, and sat enjoying a drink as if nothing had gone wrong. What the hell, Bishop thought, and poured himself two straight scotches which he drank without saying a word.

"Are you really enjoying that?" Nancy asked after Bishop tossed down his second.

"What?"

"The booze. You're drinking by rote. What's wrong?"

145

"Nothing," he shrugged, then thought a second. "I don't know. It's all so confusing."

"Just finding that out, huh?" Susan joked.

"I've only been out here a week," he protested.

"A week! How'd you get to be Major Cannon's wingman that fast?"

Bishop looked at Cannon, and felt afraid. "Just lucky, I guess," he said.

"Really, Tom . . . that's very fast work," the girl insisted.

Bishop knew why he was Cannon's wingman—because he was too new to argue. He was a good pilot, but didn't as yet have the reputation with which to challenge Cannon's questionable techniques. The thought made Bishop more sullen, so he poured himself another drink and retreated into it.

Cannon turned his attention to Ellie Kovaks, who was absorbed watching Nichols and Samantha jitterbug. "So it's you and Casey, huh?" he said.

"I'm sorry, Major?" she said, turning to him.

"Larry Casey . . . you're going with him, right?"

"Larry's mine, all right," she said.

"He's a good-looking boy," Cannon said. Then, eyeing her, "Of course, you're a good-looking woman."

"Thank you, sir."

"And smart, too. I can see that. Yeah," Cannon went on, drawing her into the conversation, "if Casey's your guy, it could have happened anywhere."

"What could have happened anywhere?" she asked.

"You two falling in love."

"I don't understand."

"Well," Cannon explained, "some people fall in love in one set of circumstances who would never fall in love under other circumstances. You know—the war, the two of you being thrown together on this island things like that."

Cannon paused a second for his words to sink in.

"But I can see you're the kind of girl who knows when her man is really in love with her and not just caught up in the circumstances, so to speak."

Ellie mulled it over as Cannon leaned back in his chair, intensely pleased with himself for having sowed the seeds of discontent in yet another quarter.

Boyington led his flight of Corsairs into Vella La Cava an hour behind Cannon's two Lightnings. The single–engine fighters taxied down to the flight line, formed up, and shut down their engines. As Boyington climbed out of his cockpit, he looked around for Micklin, and was angered to find the chief mechanic wasn't there. In fact, there wasn't a mechanic around any of the Corsairs. Scowling, Boyington looked around until he found the problem.

Micklin had the mechanics gathered in a circle around Cannon's Lightning. The cowling was off the starboard engine, and Stan Richards sat astride it with a pointer. As Micklin called off the various parts, Richards pointed them out.

"The beard radiator is sandwiched between the inter–cooler air intake and the oil radiator intake," Micklin lectured. "Remember, now, these are liquid–cooled engines. You gotta watch the coolant levels or the Major and his wingman are gonna wind up in the drink."

Micklin spotted Boyington striding toward him. "So if I'm not around when he takes off, I want you to check it. Okay," Micklin concluded, "you better go check them Corsairs."

The mechanics sprinted across the flightline as Boyington went up to Micklin.

"What the hell is going on, Andy?"

"Just a little familiarization course."

"You might try familiarizing them with a Corsair first."

"There's other things they gotta know," Micklin said.

"And there's not a chance in hell the Marine Corps will be flying P–38's. So shape up, Sergeant, and get my plane serviced. The windshield defroster's broken. I was icing up all the way back from Rabaul."

"It worked fine yesterday."

"It doesn't work today!" Boyington snapped. "And where's Jeb's plane?"

"I took it from him for not eating his cereal!" Micklin shot back, outraged. "How the hell should I know where his bird is? Go hire some divers and look for it!"

Boyington was surprised, stunned. At once, Micklin realized he'd said the wrong thing.

"You don't know?" he asked.

"Know what?"

"Pruitt didn't come back with Cannon. He got flamed over the Slot. Air-Sea picked him up, I think."

"Where's Cannon?" Boyington asked.

"The Sheep Pen, I think," Micklin said uneasily.

Boyington took off on a run and soon burst into the Sheep Pen, where Cannon was still holding court at his table. Boyington caught him as he was talking intently with Casey's girl, and knocked the beer out of his hand.

"Where's that boy?" Boyington growled.

Startled, Cannon got to his feet, clenching his fists.

"Shut that damn thing off!" Boyington yelled, pointing at the juke box. Someone pulled the plug.

"I said, where's Jeb?"

"Has something happened to Jeb?" Samantha asked, quite concerned.

"He's probably fine," Cannon said.

"Probably?" Boyington said.

"He's fine. He got picked up by a Dumbo and is

on his way to Espritos Marcos." Cannon checked his watch. "He'll be landing there in another ten minutes."

"Why didn't you say something?" Samantha said angrily.

"Because there's no way to find anything out before Air-Sea drops him on Espritos," Cannon said, regaining his composure. "I didn't want to shake you girls up."

Samantha gave Cannon a disgusted look.

"Casey," Boyington said, "get on . . ."

". . . the radio to Espritos," Casey said, breaking for the door. "Right!"

As the Black Sheep rushed out the door after Casey, Boyington stood looking at Cannon. Bishop remained in his seat.

"That boy better be okay," Boyington said. "You were supposed to see to it."

"He will be."

"Major Boyington," Bishop said. "It's not his fault. It's mine. I didn't follow orders. I . . ."

Cannon cut him off. "I was the leader," he said. "Getting Pruitt home was my job and I'll take full responsibility for it."

"But Major . . ."

"He's right, son," Boyington said, glaring at Cannon, "I'm holding you responsible."

With that, Boyington whirled and stalked out of the Sheep Pen.

Cannon turned on his wingman. "You're never gonna learn when to keep your mouth shut, are you?" he snapped.

chapter
23

GENERAL MOORE puffed hard on a small cigar while walking down the corridor which bypassed the radio room on Espritos Marcos. With the invasion of Bougainville in the late planning stages, every day was a busy one for Moore. As operational commander of all Marine fighter squadrons in that area of the Pacific, Moore was in the throes of deciding the part to be played by Vella La Cava and the Black Sheep. So when he heard Casey calling on the radio, he ducked into the radio room and took over for the Espritos Marcos operator.

"This is General Moore," he growled, "who's this?"

"Lieutenant Casey, sir."

"Get Boyington on the horn!"

"Yes, sir."

Concerned about Pruitt, the Black Sheep were pouring into the radio shack anyway. Boyington was on the radio in an instant.

"General?"

"Go ahead, Greg."

"How is Pruitt? One of my pilots . . . Jeb Pruitt . . . he got shot down this morning over the Slot . . ."

"Did Air-Sea get him?" Moore asked.

"Yeah."

"Then I can have Lard check on him and get back to you. What happened?"

"He took a few hits over Rabaul, then got flamed by a Zero on the way home," Boyington said.

"How'd you let that happen?" Moore asked.

"I stayed with the squadron and made another run on Rabaul. Two Air Force guys were supposed to escort Jeb home. Cannon and Bishop."

"Burt Cannon?"

"The same."

"I heard about those orders of his," Moore said. "Well, he's the top ace, so who can argue with him? I'll check on Pruitt, Greg. Now, let's talk about this morning's mission . . . How'd you do?"

"We hit all the destroyers in the harbor," Boyington said.

"Did you heavily damage any?"

"Don French caught one with its munitions hold open and blew it apart. If that tin can didn't sink, it never will. And it took the dock with it, too. The rest of us mainly messed up the superstructures of the others. I know I demasted one, and made a few hundred holes in the bridge."

"Greg, I want a recon mission before dark," Moore said.

"Over Rabaul?"

"If I could make it Miami Beach, I would."

"Today, sir?"

"Yes, today. I have to know if those Jap destroyers are capable of running the Slot tonight."

"Yes, sir," Boyington said, tired.

"Did you have any trouble with Zekes?"

"Not going in. Coming out it was a hornet's nest."

"Okay," Moore said. "Fly the recon mission, and make it a good one. I'll let you know when I hear about Pruitt."

General Moore signed off, then went in search of Colonel Lard. He found Lard and brought the colonel back into his office.

"Sir," Lard asked, "what's this all about?"

"Two things, Colonel. One of the Black Sheep went down in the Slot today. His name is Pruitt, and he's a lieutenant. Check on him. The other thing relates to an Army captain, Burt Cannon . . ."

"*The* Burt Cannon?"

"Yeah. Pull the file on him and give it to me. And . . ." Moore cleared his throat. ". . . not just the official file . . . *our* file, okay?"

Lard knew well what General Moore was talking about. In the course of running up his kill record, Cannon's techniques had not escaped official notice. There was no solid evidence against him, only suspicion. He'd always been given the benefit of the doubt. He was, after all, shooting down enemy planes.

Moore read the files, then went to the base hospital where Lard had determined that Lieutenant Pruitt had been taken. Pruitt was in a ward with a dozen other officers from various services, and when he saw Moore he tried to salute despite the cast on his arm.

"At ease, Lieutenant," Moore said with a laugh.

"Thank you, sir," Pruitt said, a bit embarrassed.

"I'm surprised you've even learned to salute, serving under Boyington," Moore said, helping himself to a chair alongside the bed.

"I try, sir."

"Very good. And how did you break your arm?"

"I landed on it, General. I never realized how hard water can be."

"Yeah, well, you'll learn more about crash landings before this war's over. I have quite a few lumps myself, and I've never flown combat. It was my bad luck to be a fighter pilot in peacetime. Now that the war's on, I'm too old. Now . . ." Moore lowered his voice to ensure privacy. ". . . I want you to tell me how you got shot down. Don't leave anything out."

"I took a hit from the AA over Rabaul," Pruitt said.

"Shore-based?"

"No, sir. From one of the destroyers."

"But you made it most of the way back to Vella La Cava before splashing."

"Yes, sir. Major Cannon and Lieutenant Bishop escorted me. But a couple of Zeros snuck in and got a piece of me. That was as much as my plane could take, and I went down."

"How did the Zeros get in if you had two P–38's escorting you?" Moore asked.

"I don't really know," Pruitt said. "I was talking to Major Cannon on the radio, then all of a sudden Lieutenant Bishop was shouting that there were Zekes on my tail. I didn't have time to get away. I guess Major Cannon didn't see the enemy planes."

"Uh huh," Moore said.

"I never did find out what happened after that."

"Cannon got the two Zekes."

"He sure is a great pilot, General."

"Yeah," Moore said, "a great pilot. Look, son, can you walk okay?"

"Sure thing."

"Then let's go to the radio room. Boyington won't rest until he knows you're okay. My jeep is waiting outside."

By the time Moore brought Pruitt to the radio room on Espritos Marcos, all the Black Sheep were packed into the radio shack on Vella La Cava. Captain Nichols had crammed in next to Bobby Boyle, and Cannon stood deferentially in the doorway.

"How'd you guys do?" Nichols asked.

"We got blitzed," Boyle said, "but Pappy got two on the way home."

"Twenty-four," Nichols said. He said it to himself, but Cannon overheard anyway. Boyington was keeping pace with him, a situation Cannon couldn't abide.

Moore brought Pruitt to the microphone and waited while the Espritos Marcos operator got Vella La Cava on the channel.

"General Moore?" Boyington answered. "Did you find out about Jeb?"

Pruitt took the microphone. "You aren't worried about me, are you, Major?"

A wave of relief swept over the Black Sheep. "Worried?" Boyington said with a laugh. "I just wanted to know if I needed a replacement pilot, that's all."

"Oh, yeah," Pruitt said, "I know what you mean. Hey . . . thank Major Cannon and Lieutenant Bishop for hanging around until I got picked up."

"Yeah, okay," Boyington said.

General Moore took the microphone. "Greg . . . that recon mission is important."

"Yes, sir," Boyington replied. "I'll get right on it. La Cava out."

Boyington and Samantha followed the rest of the squadron out of the radio shack. When they were out in the sunlight, Samantha gave him a kiss on the cheek. "Replacement pilot, huh?" she said.

Boyington shrugged and slipped an arm around her. "We got a bunch of fresh limes out of the jungle," he said. "Suppose I try to make you a gimlet."

"Fine with me, boss," she replied, then, seeing Major Cannon waiting for them, frowned. She intensely disliked the Air Corps ace, and separated herself from Boyington. "I'll wait for you in the Sheep Pen," she said, continuing on ahead of him.

"Right," Boyington replied.

"That's a very pretty lady," Cannon said.

"Yeah. Thanks for flying cap on Jeb after he went down."

"Forget it."

Boyington started off toward the flight line, and Cannon walked along with him.

"How about me flying that recon mission?" Cannon asked.

"I'm flying it."

"It's going to be hot over Rabaul, right?"

"Probably."

"The highest you can get is around 35,000, right?" Cannon said.

"Right."

"My Lightning can reach 45,000. The Zekes can reach you . . . but not me."

"If you fly it at 45,000," Boyington said pointedly.

Cannon stopped walking, and so did Boyington. The two aces looked at one another.

"What do you mean?" Cannon asked.

"I mean I think you'd dive on the first Zeke you saw. You'd blow the mission to run up a score. And that means I fly it."

Boyington walked off toward his plane. As he did so, Cannon glared at him, drawing himself up to full height and resting one hand menacingly on his .45.

chapter
24

ANDY MICKLIN was working with a small wire brush, cleaning coral dust out of the main spar dive flap on Cannon's Lightning when Boyington came storming up to him.

"Micklin!" he yelled. "Get away from that forked-tail bird and get a recon camera on my plane!"

"What's the matter with you, Boyington?" Micklin shot back. "You didn't wreck your plane this morning, so you want another chance?"

"Just do it, would you? And how come you're spending so much time on Cannon's plane?"

"He asked me nice," Micklin said.

"Well, I'm telling you nice. . . . Stick to your job, which is fixing Corsairs! And get going on the recon camera!"

"All right, sonny boy," Micklin snapped, waving his cigar at Boyington. "I'll do it for you! But you better bring that bird home safely! This is three times in a row you've gone out without wrecking her. Don't press your luck."

Micklin got the camera, affixed it to the belly of Boyington's Corsair, and, when the Major had taken off for Rabaul, stomped off to the mechanics' shed. He had taken about as much grief from Boyington as he could handle, and it was time for his siesta anyway. The midday sun beat down hard on the tropical island,

and while Boyington would be cool enough at 35,000 feet, Micklin was boiling.

With his heart set on a few cold beers, he walked into his office. A supply room in the back of the mechanics' shed, it held an old desk, a refrigerator filled almost exclusively with beer and a metal storage shelf loaded with tools. Lieutenant Bishop sat at the desk, his feet up on it, a beer bottle in his hand.

"Are you back?" Micklin scowled.

Bishop nodded without looking at the sergeant.

"You're drinkin' all my beer, aren't you?"

In answer, Bishop held up a ten dollar bill. Micklin plucked it from his fingers.

"That'll help," Micklin said. "It's pretty decent of you, too. Boyington never offers to pay when he takes my stuff."

Micklin fetched a beer for himself and eased down onto the floor alongside Bishop. "So what's eatin' you, kid?" he asked. "You didn't come here 'cause you like the company."

"Cannon," Bishop said.

"What about him? He seems okay to me."

"Sure. He gives you cigars. He gives me nothing but grief. And as for Jeb . . ."

"You worryin' about Pruitt?" Micklin asked. "I told you, these guys always come back. Nothin' you do to 'em makes any difference."

"It could have been prevented. Jeb didn't have to get flamed."

"He got hit by AA fire from Rabaul, right?"

"Yeah, that's what put him out of action. But he could have made it all the way back to La Cava. Except Cannon wanted to use him as bait."

Bishop told Micklin the story of how Cannon used Pruitt to draw the two Zeros into firing range. When he was finished, Micklin shook his head slowly and reached into the refrigerator for another beer.

"You know, if you tell that story to Boyington, he's gonna go crazy," Micklin said.

"You're the only one I'm gonna tell. I like living."

"Cannon's that crazy about running up a score?"

Bishop nodded.

Micklin got up from the floor and shook the kinks out of his arms. "I'll be back," he said, and walked out of the room.

Micklin found Stan Richards at the door to the mechanics' shed, poring over a P–38 air cleaner.

"Stan!"

"Yeah, Sarge?"

"Did you put a new defroster in Boyington's Corsair?" asked Micklin.

"Like you told me to, yeah."

"What was wrong with the old one?"

"The cable had a crimp in it. I swear I don't know how that happened, Sarge. It was perfect when I checked it out last week."

"What happens in one of those birds if the defroster don't work?" Micklin asked.

"Anything over 20,000 feet, the canopy frosts up. Boyington wouldn't be able to see an enemy plane if it was on top of him."

Micklin nodded gravely.

"Did I do right?" Richards asked.

"Yeah," Micklin said, deeply troubled, "you did right."

Boyington was as high as his supercharger could take him. The view from 35,000 feet was spectacular. It almost made him forget the war. He was about 80 miles out when the coast of New Britain broke upon the horizon. That meant the Japanese would be picking him up on radar at any time. He had been hoping that one lone recon plane at 35,000 feet wouldn't be deemed worth going after. He was wrong.

A flight of ten Zeros hung on their propellers as they clawed for altitude. Getting to Boyington was all that seemed to matter to them. He knew it took a long time to climb that high—even for a Zero. That was why trying to intercept him didn't seem to make much sense. But then, as Boyington finished his run and was starting to bank for home, he saw her.

Among the destroyers, cruisers and armored patrol boats in Rabaul harbor was the biggest, fattest battleship Boyington had ever seen. She was so big, she made the cruisers and destroyers around her look like canoes.

Boyington circled once, despite the rising Zeros, to take another look and grab some more photos. It wasn't every day that one got a view like that. As the Zeros moved within 5,000 feet of him, Boyington banked and headed away from Rabaul. By the time the enemy planes reached his altitude, he was long gone.

The thought of the battleship plagued him. He'd never seen anything quite so big. It was common knowledge that the Japanese had built the two biggest warships ever. But it was also believed that after Midway they kept them in home waters, away from American planes. If one was in Rabaul, it meant nothing but trouble for the allies.

Boyington wasn't back at La Cava an hour before the photo lab had his recon film developed. As he stood in the darkroom, acquainting his eyes with the red light of the safe lamp, the door opened and General Moore stepped inside. Oddly enough, Boyington wasn't surprised. Moore had a way of appearing at crucial moments.

"Greg," Moore said.

"Hello, General. I was expecting to radio you with the news."

"What news?"

"Look at this," Boyington said, indicating an 8 × 10 image of the battleship in Rabaul harbor.

"Beautiful," Moore said, squinting at the image.

"It's the Tornaga, all right."

"And still leaking oil. Five days ago, one of our subs put three torpedoes in her off the Marshalls. It didn't do much direct damage—she carries better than sixteen inches of steel armor along her sides—but she *is* losing fuel. We'd hoped she'd put into Rabaul for repairs and refueling instead of going home to Japan."

"Excuse me, General," Boyington said, "but a while ago you were worried about a couple of destroyers. Those destroyers look like canoes next to the Tornaga. Once the Japs get that mamma-san repaired, she's going to come sashaying down the Slot blowing everything out of the water, including the islands."

"Not if we get her first," Moore said eagerly.

chapter
25

SAMANTHA STOOD with her head against the wall of the Sheep Pen. Her feet were a yard away from the wall, her hands clasped behind her back. Using her head for leverage, she pushed away from the wall and stood erect without using her hands.

"That's the dumbest trick I ever saw," Bragg said.

"So, let's see you guys do it," Nancy said.

"Are you kidding?" French said.

"No."

"Anyone can do that," Bragg said.

"Sam can. Nancy can. I can. But I'll bet you two can't," Susan said.

At the word "bet" Bragg fished his wallet out of his pocket, and was about to take money out of it when Cannon stopped him.

"That's a sucker bet," Cannon said.

"Huh?"

"A woman's built different than a man."

"No kidding," Boyle laughed.

"The bulk of a woman's weight is below the waist," Cannon explained. "The bulk of a man's is above. It's simple for them to do that trick and damn near impossible for us."

Cannon and Boyle watched as Bragg and French assumed the position and tried without luck to stand.

"That's some kind of trick," Boyle said, pocketing his wallet. "Thanks . . . I owe you one."

"Forget it," Cannon said, popping open a beer and handing it to the Marine pilot. "What's a wingman for?"

"Yeah," Boyle laughed.

"How long have you been flying lead?" Cannon asked.

"I don't fly lead. I'm Casey's wingman."

"I thought I saw you flying lead this morning."

"Nope. That was Casey."

"But you switch now and then, don't you?" Cannon asked.

"What for?"

"Nothing important," Cannon said with a shrug. "Just that I let my wingman fly lead every third mission. It's good for both of us. It gives him a chance to get in lead time and reminds me how tough that rear position is to fly."

"It sounds like a good system," Boyle said, no longer sure he was happy with playing second fiddle to Casey.

As Boyle pondered, Cannon turned his attention to George Baumann. The Black Sheep's second in command had been listening to the conversation in silence. "You fly the daily patrols, right?" Cannon asked.

"We all fly daily patrols," Baumann said.

"What I mean is when Boyington leads a strike on Rabaul, you stay close to La Cava."

"Somebody has to protect the base," Baumann said.

"I guess so."

Cannon dropped the matter, preferring to let the dissension ferment in both Boyle and Baumann. Before long, Baumann turned toward him, visibly annoyed.

"I fly on the important missions too," he said.

"Of course you do."

"I mean, not recently. I was . . . unh . . . a bad boy."

"Oh?" Cannon asked.

"I got shot up by a Jap picket boat disguised as an American PT boat," Baumann said.

"Mistakes like that can happen to anyone," Cannon said. "Take me for example—I can't tell one ship from another."

"You're kidding?"

"Nope. I know what a submarine is, but that's about it."

Baumann tossed down his drink and poured himself another.

"I'd like to get that goddam Jap boat someday," he growled.

"Get even? I'm sure you will."

"If it wasn't for him, I would have gone on the Rabaul mission this morning instead of flying a routine patrol."

"Pappy got him, George," Boyle said. "Don't you remember?"

"There were two boats. Pappy only got one of them. The other one is mine."

Baumann finished another drink, stood up and walked angrily toward the door.

"See you around, Captain," Cannon said with a grin.

Casey had parked the base jeep in the small clearing where the road met the beach. This was on the Black Sheep's side of Vella La Cava, and it was a lot more isolated than the larger beach which was shared with the Navy. Casey had laid out a blanket in the sand, and was resting on it with Ellie Kovacs under his arm. The remains of a picnic lunch sat nearby. As far as he could see across the blue water, there was no sign of life—particularly, no sign of the war. Casey felt at peace with the world.

"Larry," Ellie said softly, "do you love me?"

"Of course I love you. I only told you so a dozen times today."

"If you met me, say in, Toledo . . . and there wasn't a war, would you still love me?"

"I've never been in Toledo," Casey said.

Ellie sat up and looked at him. "I'm serious," she said.

"So am I," Casey said, sitting up next to her. "What kind of questions are you asking? Toledo? Who cares about Toledo?"

"Larry," she insisted, "I want to know if we're doing what we're doing because of the war or because we're really in love."

"Because we're really in love."

"Are you sure?"

"I'm sure," Casey said. He went to kiss her, but she pulled away.

"I'm not," she said. "I have to know if you love me because you love me or if you love me because of circumstances."

"Huh?" Casey asked, bewildered.

"Aren't you listening? I want to know if you'd love me in Toledo?"

"What's with Toledo?" he asked in exasperation.

"Larry!"

"Yes," he said quickly, "I'd love you in Toledo!"

He tried to push her back down onto the blanket, but Ellie resisted.

"We are going to talk about this," she said.

Casey sighed loudly. There was nothing he could do about it, and he only wished he could understand what had gotten into her.

"Okay," he said, "let's talk." He rummaged

through the remains of the picnic lunch and was chagrined to find there was no more beer.

"Now," she went on, "if you were in Toledo, say at a dance, and there were all these girls, including me . . . who would you pick to dance with?"

"You, of course."

"What do you mean 'of course'?"

"I mean that I'm in love with *you* . . . not the other girls," Casey said.

"That's not the point!" she said sharply. "I want to know if you'd pick me! Even if you didn't know me!"

"Sure I would. I already did, didn't I? Pick you, that is."

"Yes, but on Vella La Cava, not in Toledo!"

"Jesus, Ellie," Casey snapped, "what the hell's the matter with you today?"

She jumped to her feet and walked away with Casey pursuing her.

"I want to be alone for awhile, Larry," she said. "I have to think."

"Ellie . . . please!"

"You go back to the base. I'll walk. I want to be alone."

Casey stared at her in astonishment as she walked alone down the hard sand at the edge of the water. Then he stalked up the beach to his jeep, jumped into it and roared off in the direction of the Sheep Pen.

When he got there, French and Bragg were still trying to duplicate the trick the girls had showed them and Boyle was standing at the bar watching in amusement.

"Hey, Larry," Boyles said, "where you been?"

Casey said nothing, but went straight to the bar and noisily dug a beer out of the bin.

"What are they doing?" he asked, glancing over at French and Bragg.

"Losing a bet," Boyle laughed.

Casey shook his head despairingly. Ellie's mysterious behavior had made him extremely upset. But as upset as Casey was, Boyle didn't pick up on it because of the thought that had been running through his head.

"Larry, I've been thinking," Boyle said. "How long has it been since you flew wing?"

"Huh?"

"How long since you flew wing?"

"I dunno . . . a year."

"What do you say we switch next mission?" Boyle asked. "You fly wing and I'll fly lead."

"Bob," Casey said irritably, "I'm B–flight leader. I can't lead B–flight while I'm flying your wing."

"Sure you could. I'll bet if you asked Pappy he'd say okay."

"No," Casey said angrily.

"Why not?" Boyle insisted.

Casey's temper erupted. "Because I said no! Doesn't anyone around here speak English?"

"Okay!" Boyle shouted, waving his hands to show disgust. As he did so, he accidentally knocked the beer out of Casey's hand. The two men glared at each other for an instant, then Casey threw a right. He hit Boyle on the side of the head, and the fight was on.

Boyle countered with two sharp left jabs before taking a right and getting knocked backward over a chair onto the floor. He scrambled to his feet and ran straight at Casey, grappling with him. The two men careened around the Sheep Pen, knocking over tables and chairs.

The nurses screamed and ran from the building as Boyle broke away from Casey and took a wild, round-house swing at him. He missed, and Casey landed a strong right which sent Boyle reeling out the door, where he collided with Boyington.

"What the hell's going on?" Boyington snapped as Casey ran outside to continue the fight.

Casey stopped in his tracks and looked at Boyle. As one, they answered, "I started it."

"I'm gonna finish it," Boyington growled.

"There won't be any more," Casey said.

"Yeah," Boyle agreed. "No more."

"Scram," Boyington snapped.

They scrammed, and Boyington went into the Sheep Pen. French and Bragg were setting tables and chairs up again, and Samantha was at the bar, getting Greg a beer.

"Thanks," he said, giving her a polite slap on the rump as reward. "What got into Casey and Bragg?"

"I think one Major Burt Cannon," she replied. "Maybe I'm way off base, but I know he's been feeding a bunch of bull to Ellie. And five minutes before the fight started he was bending Bobby's ear. I don't care if he is America's leading ace and a big hero. I don't like him."

Boyington shrugged.

"God knows what he told George," she concluded.

"What?"

"Yeah, and George really took off afterward. He looked pretty ticked off."

chapter
26

STAN RICHARDS looked up at Boyington's Corsair with considerable surprise. Micklin had never before shown particular interest in Boyington's plane. In fact, he seemed at times almost willing to avoid working on it at all. But suddenly Micklin seemed obsessed with the plane.

"What do you want me to do, Sarge?" Richards asked, waving a handful of tools.

"I want you to get up into that cockpit," Micklin said, "and go over everything."

"Everything, Sarge?"

"Yeah! Everything that could get broken by accident. All the instruments, everything."

"I did that this morning," Richards protested.

"Do it again this afternoon! I don't want to hear it from Boyington if something goes wrong with this bird!"

"Sure thing," Richards said, climbing up into the cockpit.

"And when you're done, I want you to make sure this plane isn't out of your sight until Boyington needs it again."

"What? Stay up all night with it?"

"As long as *somebody* keeps an eye on it," Micklin said.

"What's the matter, Sarge?"

"Nothing. Just do like I told you. I don't have

time to stand around here jawin' with you. I got things to do."

"You gonna go back to work on the P–38?" Richards asked.

"No," Micklin said, turning and stalking off.

Richards disappeared into the cockpit of the Corsair and began a systematic checkout of the several dozen controls and instruments. Micklin stomped off in the direction of the reserve Corsair he had been working on when Cannon first came to Vella La Cava. Micklin had thought for a time about rearranging Cannon's face. But then, he had no hard evidence that Cannon had sabotaged Boyington's Corsair by messing up the defroster. It was, though, exactly the sort of thing a pilot would think of sabotaging. The damage wouldn't be obvious until way too late, and if Boyington were shot down as a result of poor visibility, there would be no way to place blame. Taken with Bishop's account of the last mission, Micklin felt some sort of retribution was in order. However, beating up on America's number one ace didn't strike him as a smart thing to do. He knew that Cannon was only staying on La Cava a few days. If he could keep him from doing further harm until then, the problem would be solved.

Micklin had the cowling off the reserve Corsair, and was just putting a wrench to one of the oil lines when Boyington ran up.

"Don't get on me, Boyington," he growled. "I'm gettin' back to work on the Corsairs."

"It isn't that. Where is Baumann's plane?"

"If it ain't under Baumann," Micklin said, "then that boy's shark bait."

"He took off?"

"About fifteen minutes ago."

"Not again!" Boyington exclaimed. "Which way did he go?"

Micklin pointed toward the southwest.

"Kolombangara," Boyington said, running off to his plane and chasing Stan Richards out of the cockpit.

Within minutes Boyington was airborne, gaining altitude and feeling a great sense of *déja vu*. Baumann had been drinking, and something Cannon told him had put the idea in his head to get revenge. But revenge against what? Kolombangara had been cleared of Japanese. Any ships in the area were bound to be Allied.

As he poured on the coal in an attempt to reach Baumann, Boyington switched on the radio and activated his throat mike.

"Black Sheep One to Black Sheep Two . . . come in, George." There was no reply, so he repeated the message. "Come on, George . . . respond!"

"Leave me alone, Greg," was the angry reply.

"You're drunk," Boyington said. "You can't go taking on the whole Japanese Navy. Return to base, George. That's an order."

Baumann muttered an obscenity.

"You're in enough trouble already," Boyington went on. "If you turn back to La Cava right now, I think I can save your skin."

"So long, Greg," Baumann said, and shut off the radio.

Boyington tried several other channels, but Baumann wasn't listening. The angry executive officer had reached the jungle island and had begun to circle, looking for the enemy. Circling ate up time. By the time Baumann found a target, Boyington was a scant few miles behind.

As Boyington watched in horror, Baumann peeled off and dived on a small warship cruising slowly just off the northern coast of Kolombangara. Uselessly, Boyington hit his mike.

"She's American, George! Break off! She's one of ours!"

Boyington was unable to stop him. As the Corsair

opened up on the PT boat, a sailor waved frantically, trying to warn Baumann off. The sailor was cut down in a hail of .50mm bullets, and at the same time, the stern gunner in the PT boat returned fire, perhaps by instinct. Boyington could do nothing but watch as Baumann's Corsair burst into flames, pulled up slightly, then crashed in the thick jungle of Kolombangara.

"It isn't your fault," General Moore said, sitting on an ironwood log near a dirt revêtement at one end of the La Cava strip.

"I should have seen it happening," Boyington said.

"No. If Baumann was intent on killing himself, there's nothing you could have done that would have made any difference."

"I could have kept the plane locked up."

"Greg . . .they're warplanes, not Model T's. It isn't that simple."

Moore took a slug of scotch straight from the bottle and passed it over to Boyington.

"I'll have to write his folks," said Boyington.

"There's never been any way to make that job easy," Moore said. "Do the best you can."

"And when I get some time I want to see if I can con one of the PT boys from the other side of the island to taking me over to Kolombangara. I think he ought to be buried."

"Sure," Moore nodded. "But for the time being, we've got something more important to do."

"The Tornaga," Boyington said.

"I want you to fly escort for a torpedo and dive–bomber mission to be launched by the Lexington. The Lex pilots requested your unit, by the way. You'll get specifics tomorrow morning."

"I didn't know the Lexington was in the area."

"She isn't. But ever since you took that picture of the Tornaga, the Lex has been making full steam in an effort to get here. Make no mistake about it. We want that Jap battlewagon out of the way. So far, they've been cautious about committing her. If the war keeps going against them, our Nipponese friends may change their minds. You know the Tornaga carries 18–inch guns?"

"I heard."

"She's the biggest and most powerful battleship ever built by any Navy. Even the Royal Navy has never come close. We want her bad, Greg."

Boyington nodded and handed back the bottle of scotch. "And as for Cannon . . ."

"Major Cannon is a talented pilot with one big need to make a name for himself," Moore said. "I've done a little research on this guy, and some things in our file show that certain of his methods are, shall we say, questionable."

"I'm pretty sure he's been filling my guys' heads with all sorts of ideas—spreading dissension. I know he started one fight, and he may have been the one who got Baumann riled up this afternoon. If that's the case . . ."

"If that's the case," Moore stepped in, "you can do something about it *after* tomorrow's mission."

"Fair enough," Boyington said.

chapter
27

AT NIGHTFALL Cannon sat in his tent, playing with his .45, aiming it at various objects. Every so often he would aim it at Lieutenant Bishop, who was unnerved enough as things stood.

"I know you've told me to stay off the radio when we're in combat," Bishop said, "but in flight school they said that the radio was . . ."

"Look, kid," Cannon cut in angrily, "I don't care what they said in flight school. How many of those stateside wife stealers are aces, huh?"

"I . . . I don't know, sir."

"How many of 'em have twenty-seven kills?" Cannon aimed the .45 at the tent pole.

"None, sir."

"You're damn right," he said, pulling the trigger. The unloaded automatic made a hollow click. "There are none! Out here is where you learn to score, not shooting at some rag target over California. You're real lucky to be my wingman, kid, you know that."

"Yes, sir," Bishop said nervously.

"You want to stay my wingman?" Cannon asked, aiming the gun at Bishop.

"Yes, sir," Bishop said.

Cannon lowered the .45. "Okay," he said, "it's real simple. I do the talking. I do the leading. I do the shooting, okay?"

"Yes, sir."

Bishop had been looking down at the floor, and when Boyington pushed his way into the tent, was delighted with the interruption.

"Son, why don't you get a little air?" Boyington said.

"Yes, sir," Bishop said, relieved to be let out of the tent.

Boyington walked to the tent pole, leaned on it and watched Cannon as the Air Corps major continued to sight his .45 on various objects in the tent.

"How'd your recon mission go?" Cannon asked.

"I got the pictures," Boyington said.

"Did you get intercepted?"

Boyington nodded.

"Get any?" Cannon asked.

Boyington didn't reply, and Cannon flashed a grin at him.

"You got blitzed, right?"

"Yeah," Boyington said. "I guess according to your rules I got blitzed. Look, Cannon, we're not in a contest. No one's handing out prizes."

"Don't be naive," Cannon laughed. "That's exactly what we're in—a contest. The ace that comes out of this war number one is gonna walk away with it all. And that's gonna be me."

"Maybe. But no flying off this rock. I want you out of here in the morning."

"You're forgetting my orders."

"I don't give a damn about your orders. Or your score. Or who goes home with the blue ribbon. In the 48 hours you've been here, my hottest pilot has gone down, my exec's gotten himself killed, one of my pilots has tangled with his wingman and my line chief has a sore elbow from polishing your bird. I want you gone, mister!"

"Okay," Cannon said, waving a .45 at Boyington,

"but remember one thing—I'm coming out of this war number one and anyone who doesn't believe that is gonna get hurt!"

"If you don't stop waving that gun at me," Boyington growled, "I'm gonna put it where it'll take a surgeon to remove it." Cannon glared at Boyington, but lowered the gun. "In the morning . . . gone!" Boyington said as he turned and walked out of the tent.

When he was gone, Cannon once again lifted the .45. He aimed it at the door and imagined himself pulling the trigger.

Dawn had barely broken over Vella La Cava when General Moore started off the briefing. The Black Sheep sat clustered around a map of New Britain and several aerial photos of Rabaul harbor, including the one showing the Tornaga which Boyington had taken.

"The Tornaga is our target, men," Moore said. "She's the sister ship of the Yamoto, and she's eight hundred and sixty feet long, has sixteen inches of armor on her sides, and carries nine 18–inch guns, twelve 6–inch guns, twenty-four 5–inch antiaircraft guns and one hundred and forty-seven—that's right, one hundred and forty-seven—one–inch AA guns."

"How the hell are we gonna make a dent in *that?*" Boyle asked.

"A lot of trying and anywhere from six to ten torpedoes should do it. Now the Navy boys will carry the torpedoes. It will be up to you to keep the Zeros off 'em long enough for them to do their jobs."

"One hundred forty-seven one–inch guns," Boyle said.

"And twenty-four five–inch guns," Moore said, "all of them with blast shields."

"Terrific," Boyington said.

"I know, Greg, but this is a job that has to be done. And this is how it's gonna work. We're sending in a squadron of bombers from Henderson. The bombers will go in high purely as a diversion. We know the Japanese will send up everything with wings to intercept them. That's just what we want. The bombers are a decoy. During the night, the Navy moved the Lexington into a position off Santa Isabel. That's well within striking range of Rabaul. Torpedo and dive bombers from her will come in under the radar. With Rabaul's Zeros up to intercept the bombers and with the Tornaga's AA men engaged in high–altitude fire, the planes from the Lexington should blow the Tornaga out of the water.

"The bombers have requested that the 214 fly escort. Once the carrier planes make their attack, the bombers will break for home. And then you guys ought to have a field day."

Moore stepped away from the maps and grinned. "Good luck and good hunting," he said.

As the Black Sheep made a rendezvous with the B–25's from Guadalcanal and continued on to Rabaul, Boyington thought about Major Cannon. The Air Corps ace wasn't at the morning briefing and the two P–38's still stood on the flight line when the Black Sheep took off, but Boyington expected Cannon to put in an appearance anyway. It was too big a show for him not to want a part of.

And it *was* a big show. Twenty minutes out of Rabaul, what looked like the entire Japanese air force rose to meet them. At least 100 Zeros, each one emblazoned with the "angry red meatball" emblem of Imperial Japan, scrambled for altitude as the B–25's and Corsairs moved in on the Tornaga.

"It looks like Moore's plan is working," Don French said.

"Yeah, but does it have to work that good?" Boyle replied.

Boyington activated his throat microphone.

"Casey . . . take B–flight and hit 'em. I'll hold A–flight here to catch what breaks through. Remember, our job is keep 'em off the bombers."

"Amen, little brother, amen," the bomber squadron leader observed.

First Casey's flight and then Boyington's tangled with the Zeros. Practicing the team flying they had made into a fine art, the Black Sheep kept the enemy fighters off the B–25's for the entirety of the first run. On the way out, only three out of the flight of 40 Zekes got through the Black Sheep. As they withdrew from the scene, Boyington looked down and watched the planes from the Lexington sweep in low and attack the battleship.

Caught entirely off guard, three torpedoes exploded against the port beam of the Tornaga before that ship's AA gunners reset for the new targets. It took ten torpedoes in all before the huge battlewagon listed so far to port that the water pouring into her overwhelmed her ability to counterflood. She rolled over and sank in less than a minute, taking most of her complement of 3,000 men with her. The Black Sheep were around long enough to see the huge ship go under before they turned tail and fled from the overwhelming number of Zeros.

"Black Sheep Leader," the bomber leader radioed, "it looks like the Navy got through! Little Beaver's taking his Indians home. Good luck and thanks."

"Roger," Boyington said, and turned his attention to his squadron. "The bombers are clear . . . Let's see if these rice balls want to hang around and play."

Finally unleashed after weeks of carefully controlled flying, the Black Sheep turned on the Japanese planes like wolves. With the bombers gone, the Black Sheep began to score heavily. Boyington seemed unable to do wrong. He flamed two Zeros in a row. Cutting across their flight paths from the side, he found them in his sights for split seconds each as if they were gifts It often happened that way in air combat. Targets wandered into a pilot's sights and were flamed in less time than it took to think about it. The third wasn't much harder. A Jap had gotten onto Casey's tail and Boyington just happened to be in the right spot to remove him.

As the combat went on, Cannon and Bishop swept in, their P–38's strangely out of place in the teeming sea of Corsairs and Zeros. A pair of Zeros were chasing Boyington. They had heard his name on the radio, and the price of fame was being a popular target.

The two Lightnings swept in behind the two Zekes chasing Boyington. Cannon set his sights on the target ahead. It was an odd thing, looking through the sights and seeing both the Zero and Boyington's Corsair. Rapt, Cannon swung his sights from one to the other and saw both clearly. It would have been as easy for Cannon to shoot down Boyington as to get the enemy pilot who was pursuing him.

Thoughts of Boyington ran through Cannon's head. The Marine ace was but one kill behind him; another five minutes and Boyington might be ahead. Cannon fixed his sights on the Corsair's tail. He was so absorbed in thinking about Boyington that he failed to see Bishop's frantic hand signals.

"A Jap on your tail!" Bishop shouted into the microphone.

There was a short burst of fire as both Cannon and the Japanese pilot chasing him opened up. Tracers cut long arcs through the air as holes appeared in the tail of the Corsair and the Lightning was ripped apart. The port boom of the P–38 separated from the tail section and it went tail over nose, spinning to a fiery death thousands of feet below.

Seething with fury, Bishop swung his plane into a

tight turn and blasted the Zero at such close range he barely saw the enemy plane catch fire and plummet. Then he swung back and got one of the Zeros on Boyington's tail as Boyle and Casey picked off the other.

"Bishop . . . is that you?" Boyington radioed.

But Bishop was looking down at the spot in the sea where Cannon's plane had crashed. "I can't believe he's gone," Bishop said.

chapter
28

BOYINGTON AND BISHOP walked slowly on their way to the flightline. Refueled and rearmed, Bishop's P–38 stood alone, apart from the Corsairs. On the side of the cockpit, beneath Bishop's name, were two kill flags. Micklin had put them on as a going-away present to the young pilot, who was returning to Espritos Marcos for reassignment.

"I'm going to take them off when I get back to Espritos," Bishop said. "I understand in this case it doesn't pay to advertize."

"No, it doesn't," Boyington agreed.

"When I think of how many he had . . ."

"Don't," Boyington interrupted. "Don't think of numbers. This isn't a ball game. Cannon wouldn't learn that lesson, and he died as a result."

"He'd be alive today if I had used the radio earlier. But he told me not to. He wanted to sneak up on the Zeros chasing you without alerting them."

"That's bull, Lieutenant. The Japanese aren't usually on the same channel as us, and what makes you think they speak English any better than we speak Japanese? Cannon didn't want to alert *me!* If I'd known about the two Zekes chasing me, I'd have dived away and loused up his chance to up his score."

"Maybe," Bishop said. "Still . . . if I'd warned

him . . . I was his wingman . No matter what he said, I should have known better."

"You tried to warn him."

"Yeah, when it was too late."

"Then you took on two Zeros at point-blank range," Boyington continued. "Very few people pull a stunt like that and live to talk about it. Son . . . you didn't kill him. In a way, those Zekes didn't even kill him. Whatever was driving Cannon started long before you two ever met. I want you to remember that."

"Yes, sir," Bishop said, brightening.

The two men came to Bishop's P–38, stood, and shook hands.

"Thank you, Major," Bishop said. "I won't forget you . . . or the Black Sheep."

"If you ever think of becoming a Marine, there's a place for you here," Boyington said.

"I'll think about it," Bishop said, and climbed up into his cockpit. Before long he was zooming down the runway and up into the sky.

Boyington walked back toward the Sheep Pen, where General Moore and an afternoon spent over beer and tall tales awaited him. But as he walked past the line of Corsairs in for repair, Micklin accosted him. The sergeant had a small lump of metal, and was tossing it up in the air and catching it again.

"You know," he said, "there's a bunch of holes in the tail of your plane."

"I know that," Boyington replied.

"Yeah, well did you also know they didn't come from no Zero."

"What?"

"And no Corsair, either. This is one of the slugs that made 'em. It's a little beaten up but still easy enough to figure out. This is the ammo the Air Corps loads in to P–38's."

Micklin handed Boyington the slug.

"Just patch up the holes and forget 'em," Boyington said with a sigh as he continued on his way toward the Sheep Pen.

A Marine corps transport brought Jeb Pruitt home in time to catch the party in the Sheep Pen. The party went on all afternoon and into the night. By the time it broke up, nearly everyone in the unit had drunk enough to carry him over through the following day, which, thankfully, they had off. Boyington retired to his tent to resume his nightly struggle with Meatball for possession of the cot, and Boyle fell asleep wondering if he'd ever manage to teach Rock to box.

At about two in the morning, when everyone was asleep, there came a familiar droning. Washing Machine Charlie was back. He hadn't bothered them in some time, and some of the Black Sheep had allowed themselves to form the impression he had gone for good.

The bomber came in low from the northeast, its two engines far enough out-of-synch to rattle the tent poles in the Marine encampment. Micklin ran out of his tent and emptied his automatic at the sky, swearing a blue streak. The rest of the Black Sheep did the same. Even Boyington managed to empty an M1 at the Japanese bomber.

"Pappy," Casey said, "doesn't the Army have a radar–equipped P–38?"

"I think so."

"If we could get one for a few nights, we could tail that bum. We could be up in the air waiting for him."

"No more P–38's," Boyington said, "I've developed a dislike for those fork–tailed birds." He walked back into his tent.

ABOUT THE AUTHOR

MICHAEL JAHN is a freelance writer and novelist who has published more than twenty novels and novelizations, including *The Six Million Dollar Man*, *The Rockford Files*, *Switch* and his own *The Quark Maneuver* and *Killer on the Heights*. In addition, he has novelized four teleplays from the *Black Sheep Squadron* television series, which have been published as *Devil in the Slot* and *The Hawk Flies on Sunday*. Mr. Jahn lives with his wife and son in New York where he writes for *The New York Times* and other major periodicals.

JOIN THE 633 SQUADRON

The original 633 SQUADRON, written a number of years ago, has become a classic of air literature, translated into many languages. The British author, Frederick E. Smith, had not planned any further books until he was deluged with reader inquiries from all over the world asking for more information about the members of this Yorkshire-based Special Service Unit. He finally was persuaded to continue the series of books about this legendary Mosquire Squadron of the RAF. The results are rousing, action-filled stories which are now being published in the United States for the first time.

633 SQUADRON

The mission was called Vesuvius, and the invasion of Europe depended on it. The squadron's target was a Norwegian fiord where Germans were developing something so secret that even the RAF crews were told nothing about it. But everyone knew this was a dangerous, almost suicidal, mission. Caught between the attacking German aircraft and the grim mountain walls, the 633 Squadron plunged into the howling valley of death.

633 SQUADRON: OPERATION RHINE MAIDEN

Under the young, brilliant, new Commander Ian Moore, the squadron flew a mission to thwart the new German anti-aircraft rocket which posed the most deadly threat to Allied invasion plans. The squadron had to come in on a daylight bombing run to wipe out the rocket factory and strike an underground target buried deep in a Bavarian valley.

633 SQUADRON: OPERATION CRUCIBLE

Autumn 1943. To restore world confidence in the RAF, which had been blamed by a British correspondent for heavy U.S. losses over Europe, the RAF and the 8th Air Force top brass chose the 633 Squadron to perform their most hazardous mission yet—giving ground support to American troops going in on a daring Dieppe-style landing against totally unforseen odds.

633 SQUADRON: OPERATION VALKYRIE

February 1944. The squadron was called on to destroy a large consignment of heavy water being smuggled out of Norway to Germany. To succeed in this mission seemed impossible until Intelligence Officer Frank Adams came up with a bizarre scheme—the only hitch was that it would put the entire squadron in great peril.

Join the Allies on the Road to Victory
BANTAM WAR BOOKS

These action-packed books recount the most important events of World War II. Specially commissioned maps, diagrams and illustrations allow you to follow these true stories of brave men and gallantry in action.

12884	ABANDON SHIP! Newcomb	$2.25
12657	AS EAGLES SCREAMED Burgett	$2.25
*12658	BIG SHOW Clostermann	$2.25
13014	BRAZEN CHARIOTS Crisp	$2.25
12666	COAST WATCHERS Feldt	$2.25
*12664	COCKLESHELL HEROES Lucas-Philips	$2.25
12916	COMPANY COMMANDER MacDonald	$2.25
*12669	ENEMY COAST AHEAD Gibson	$2.25
*12927	THE FIRST AND THE LAST Galland	$2.25
*11642	FLY FOR YOUR LIFE Forrester	$1.95
13572	GUERRILLA SUBMARINES Dissette & Adamson	$2.25
13121	HELMET FOR MY PILLOW Leckie	$2.25
12663	HORRIDO! Toliver & Constable	$2.25

*Cannot be sold to Canadian Residents.

Buy them at your local bookstore or use this handy coupon:

Bantam Books, Inc., Dept. WW2, 414 East Golf Road, Des Plaines, Ill. 60016

Please send me the books I have checked above. I am enclosing $_____
(please add $1.00 to cover postage and handling). Send check or money order
—no cash or C.O.D.'s please.

Mr/Mrs/Ms _____

Address _____

City _____ State/Zip _____

WW2—4/80

Please allow four to six weeks for delivery. This offer expires 10/80.

RELAX!
SIT DOWN
and Catch Up On Your Reading!